I0831903

Jaffer vs Sharief

Jaffer vs Sharief

Unnikrishnan Cheruthuruthy

Foreword by
C.K. JAFFER SHARIEF

RUPA

Published by
Rupa Publications India Pvt. Ltd 2015
7/16, Ansari Road, Daryaganj
New Delhi 110002

Sales Centres:
Allahabad Bengaluru Chennai
Hyderabad Jaipur Kathmandu
Kolkata Mumbai

This is a work of fiction. Names, characters, places and incidents are either the product of the author's imagination or are used fictitiously and any resemblance to any actual person, living or dead, events or locales is entirely coincidental.

ISBN: 978-81-291-3851-4

First impression 2015

10 9 8 7 6 5 4 3 2 1

Dedicated to
Bhaskaramenon Krishnakumar alias Aatmaaraaman
one with a gifted pen, but self-imprisoned…

CONTENTS

Foreword *ix*

Janus Faced 1
Down Family Lane 4
Tipu Sultan 10
Introspection 15
The Court 19
Under that Banyan Tree 23
Rejection, Separation and Reunion 27
The Villain Photograph 32
God's Own Voice 39
Advaita 43
Concepts of Charity and Beauty 47
Protocol 51
Scorpio 56
Interview 60
Tragedy 66
Polygamy 69
Matinee 72
Wedding Anniversary 74
Female Fraternity 77
She Is No More 82
Battle of Wits 85
Adieu to Amina Bi 88

Last Rites 91
Mea Culpa 93
Ahimsa 97
Hoofprints and Pugmarks 100
Pisciculture 104
Male Chauvinism 108
Offshoots 111
Fakir 116
Nadi Reading 119
Chikamagalur 123
Lal Bagh 127
Foreigner 131
Matriculate 135
Blind God 139
A Divine Visitor 141
Royal Feast 143
On that Friday... 145
A Much Maligned Soul 148
Dreams 152
Diplomacy 157
Wrong/Wronged 162
Advice 164
Fate Strikes Again 166
Dialogue Underground 171
Cross-examination 174
Memories Revisited 177
He Too... 181
Judgment 184
Farewell 186

Acknowledgements 188

FOREWORD

HAVING BEEN ONE OF my associates for close to half a century, the author is not a stranger to me. Yet, I am not confident enough to declare that I know him. He seems at once to be very near as well as far away. Indeed, he is reverential to me in my presence, but I wouldn't be surprised if he turned a critic behind my back. I have observed a shade of cynicism in his approach to men and matters, yet, I would not call him a universal cynic. Our association has been marked by an undulating topography of love, hate and indifference, but its crest is one of mutual understanding. We have survived several bouts of divergence and uncertainty. With each episode of crisis or conciliation, we resolved never to meet again or never to part again as the case may have been. After all, life is like that.

Over the years, several people have approached me, asking to write my biography. All of them were not necessarily fascinated by my past. Yet, I did not discourage them. By and large, each one has a Narcissus in one's ego! I am no different. The moment I yielded, the other would start claiming my time and asking me to share my memories. A few of them have brought out their works too, which are varied and variegated in comprehension and presentation of the subject. There is a saying that no two persons see one rainbow or bathe in the same river. Analogous to that theory, no two biographers write about one person. But, they did have one thing in common—all were benign in highlighting my virtues.

Like other authors, I believed that Unnikrishnan Cheruthuruthy, the author of *Jaffer vs Sharief*, would also come to me for information. But he did not. I then concluded that perhaps he already had enough material in his custody, as our companionship had been a long one. Then he came and announced that the manuscript was ready. As he proceeded with his narration, I was amused to learn that he was not writing my story; rather, he was writing fiction under the title of my name. According to him, my name had the potential for enormous imaginings. As for the title, he uses a split version of my name. All this left me stupefied. A cursory reading of the sample chapters that he showed me left me terribly embarrassed. In fact, he was attributing all his wilder and out of this world imaginings to me. The first time, I took him to be a dishonest person, a distortionist and a fabricator. I asked him why I should own up to all his fallacies. He argued with me and said that what he had written was not my story at all; instead, he was building up a story to suit my name. To my query as to why he should seek my consent (since my name is not the rarest of rare names), he meekly sought my permission to colourize and use a few situations and sequences from my life, purely for drama. Though I enjoyed his discomfiture, I politely vetoed the project lock, stock and barrel, reminding him that I was not a soft target for his literary fantasies. That resulted in a spell of separation which, by then, was long overdue.

After a three-year silence one misty morning, he knocked on my door. I welcomed him warmly. Gradually, the topic of his manuscript came up. He obviously wanted to test whether I was still resolute in my earlier stand, or had mellowed. I, who had forgotten all he had made me read in the past, perhaps involuntarily, displayed a sort of watered-down dissent over the issue. Exploiting that opportunity, he unleashed a long lecture, which in brief went as follows:

As a typical Jaffer Sharief, you possess contradictory

emotions like love for virtue and hatred for greed, sacrifice of valuables and possessiveness of the trivial, religiosity in faith and secularism in conviction, compassion for the weak and intolerance for the lazy, admiration for beauty and disdain for the careless, a taste for the urban and nostalgia for the rural, and the like. A person who has your attitude to life should not worry about what others think of him. You have nothing to hide from society. You are a person much misunderstood by the indifferent and gullible. *Jaffer vs Sharief* offers a chance for the world to learn that here is a character, resembling, though faintly and distantly, you. This character is constantly in communion, and mostly in harmony, with his conscience. You have been subjected to several allegations, controversies, blackmail and mudslinging of various natures by your detractors. Yet, the heavens did not fall on your head. Disagreement over publication of this work is tantamount to throttling an attempt to fictionalize a philosophical life that is, here and there, similar to yours. You are not orthodox, you are not fearful, you are not shy…

When the guest stopped for breath, I, eager to escape from his tirade, jumped at the chance, intervened and asked him what he wanted. He said he wanted my consent to publish his fiction, with my name in the title.

I said, 'All right, go ahead!'

C.K. Jaffer Sharief
Bengaluru

JANUS FACED

HEY, SHADE, DO YOU recognize me?

Oh, of course I do, Shine. After all, I am your other self. You had given me the challenging assignment of keeping track of Challakare Kareem Jaffer Sharief for over three-quarters of a century.

Well, I do remember. So, what's your conclusion?

I see in him two different people—it's almost as if it's Jaffer *vs* Sharief.

That's funny!

Yes. At times, Jaffer overpowers Sharief; at others, Sharief conquers Jaffer. While Sharief floats among clouds of loftier otherworldly ideals, Jaffer crawls through casual sensuous dreams. One yearns to listen to a big bang in the vast expanse of silent ignorance, the other conducts research to discover a black hole of solitude in the battlefield of knowledge. One is possessive even about a ballpoint pen, the other denies himself kingdoms and knighthoods. While one is concerned with the concept of time, the other shows scant respect for essential punctuality.

Life then must be a constant conflict.

Not always. There are instances when they agree to a ceasefire and live in harmony. At such times, few can match or catch up with the unified Jaffer Sharief. In such a state, he can scale dazzling heights and remain on top of the world. In fact, he becomes a miniature version of Archimedes, who said, 'If I have a lever to hold and a place to stand, I will move the earth.'

You are right, Shade. When you pronounce the name, Jaffer Sharief, it sounds like the flapping wings of a soaring bird.

But Shine, in the next moment he stage-manages a precipitous fall, head over heels into a bottomless pit. On certain occasions, the words 'Jaffer Sharief' are reminiscent of a railway engine gasping for breath as it chugs to its terminal. In his name, 'J' seems to stand for friction and sparks and 'S' for a sort of dousing effect. It is a combination of inflammation and reconciliation.

Shade, your observation is interesting. Either the name followed the person or the person the name. Those who selected the name, sure enough, were guided by certain transcendental signals. In brief, our hero possesses a complex personality. By the way, have you drawn out a balance sheet of his aggressions and retreats, conquests and defeats, agonies and ecstasies?

I have his statistics at my fingertips.

Well, get ready.

But Shine, how many Homo sapiens are free from the affliction of dual personality?

True, you've hit the bull's eye! I shall answer your question with an example from Vedic philosophy. Two birds live in one tree; they are inseparable friends. One eats the fruits that the tree yields. The other watches him without eating. In this case, the tree represents the body and the birds, the two selves within each individual. The one that does not eat the fruit is the absolute self while the one that does, is the relative self. Thus, the relative self experiences joy and sorrow, while the absolute self just watches; the relative self is engaged while the absolute self is uninvolved. Thus goes the ancient allegory.

But Shine, the yield of a particular tree need not necessarily be nourishing and delicious?

No, it can be sweet, sour or bitter, raw, ripe or rotten. Now, listen, how about an experiment? Sharief can be a metaphor for the absolute self while Jaffer can be representative of the relative self. If they occasionally violate the boundaries, we'll ignore it, since the mantles are not tailor-made for them.

Agreed, but Jaffer Sharief is fussy about the fit of his outfits.

Never mind, after all the beholder will be the judge.

Well.

Then bring him.

Okay Shine. Few have a history worth recording and our hero is one among those few. His life, sans prejudice or predilection, could serve as an inspiring guide to ignite creativity in future generations. Are we bent upon a ruthless dissection?

Yes, Shade. Hold him tight and pin him down.

Anaesthesia?

No. He is strong enough to withstand the pains of introspection.

Oh, God! He has slipped away from my grip!—Shade cried

How come?

A call for the Magrib prayer from the nearby green-painted mosque rescued him.

This is the intervention of nature, it ordains, 'Don't harass my child; he is my darling.'

We should abide by the laws of the heavens.

Shine, it is worthwhile to undertake a journey to trace the footprints of his forefathers. Let's begin with a visit to his grandchild's school tomorrow.

That is a good idea. The slanting rays of the evening sun drag me westward. See you tomorrow, goodnight!

Goodnight!

DOWN FAMILY LANE

SHADE, I AM AFRAID Jaffer Sharief will not emerge before we return from his grandson's school. He is a person who does not compromise on protocol privileges. I am his pilot and you are the escort.

Today, he will take time to get up. Last night, he took a double dose of Larpose. Do you remember the first day when he moved out with the pilot and the escort provided by the state?

Indeed! Shine recollected the event quite clearly and repeated the proceedings:

'I,' the President of the Republic prompted, in his effeminate voice, the oath of office to the young member, who picked up the words and read nonstop, unmindful of punctuations: 'I Jaffer Sharief do hereby solemnly affirm in the name of God that I will… I will not…' When he finished reading, he shook hands with the head of the nation, moved to a side table, signed the register and alighted from the platform. He suddenly remembered that he had forgotten to take back his pen, but decided to forsake it. Instead he paid obeisance to the lady Prime Minister and returned to a third row seat.

After the session, he was surrounded by the media.

'Sir, what is foremost in your mind now?'

'One Independence Day, when I was in the seventh class, the deputy commissioner of the district had come to hoist the national flag in our village panchayat. We, schoolchildren were made to stand around the flag post. I mistook a man in a red turban and wide belt for the deputy commissioner. He was, in fact, his ceremonial peon. From this moment, a man with a similar uniform escorts me. I with my wrinkled kurta and pajama, could easily be taken for a menial by many.'

'Yes, your simplicity has been noted—no bandgala or sherwani. We watched several guests admiring you.'

'But friends, I get the credit by default. The invitation did not reach me, as my phone was dead for two days. I entered the hall only to witness the swearing-in of others. Strange are the ways of providence. I was not only included in the council of ministers, but was accommodated at a higher level also.'

The next day, in one of the vernacular newspapers, a cartoon appeared with the caption: 'the midwife who came for the delivery instead delivered twins!'

I remember—Shade added:

That night Jaffer Sharief could not close his eyes. Lying in bed, he was figuring out his forefathers. In that process, at the confluence of the last day's last moment and the next day's first moment, his wakefulness evaporated into oblivion like a fading shadow of an unknown little bird far in the late evening horizon.

We reached the school. This is Jaffer Sharief's grandson's class. Let us position ourselves closer to the ventilator and watch the class:

'Boys today, I will test your capacity to walk back along the corridors of your main family lane. You should name your forefathers. Let me see who can go back the furthermost.' It was a history class and the teacher called each student one by one.

First row is over. Many children could not go beyond their fathers. Few could recollect the name of their grandfathers. One stood up and, true to his nature, took a few seconds to start.

'You don't even remember your dad's name?' the teacher remarked.

'Ma'am, he wants a clue!' A backbencher commented and the whole class laughed.

'Now, come on Wahab,' the teacher turned to the boy in the corner.

'You are the son of?'

'Abdul Kareem Sharief.'

'Grandson of?'

'Jaffer Sharief.'

'Great-grandson of?'

'Abdul Kareem.'

'Great-great-grandson of?'

'Abdul Lateef.'

'Great-great-great-grandson of?'

'Abdul Usman!'

'Brilliant sense of history; keep it up. You have linked yourself to your sixth ancestor.'

'Further back?'

'Nothing is visible. It is pitch dark.'

'So you have reached the rock bottom. But, you could excavate the depth of your past like ...'

'...a boring bandicoot,' the backbencher helped complete the teacher's sentence.

'A cute parallel with an apt adjective, yet it betrays a streak of mischief.' The teacher turned to the boy again.

'Can you visualize all your forefathers?'

The boy responded like one hypnotized.

'Not beyond Jaffer Sharief. I have not seen Abdul Kareem or Abdul Lateef or Abdul Usman even in photos. But they say that my father Abdul Kareem is a replica of his grandfather, Abdul Kareem. The resemblance is striking. The similarity does not end with appearance alone. My father's signature is mysteriously similar to that of my great-grandfather. My grandfather, Jaffer Sharief, uses his son's—my father's—photo as his caller ID for his mobile phone. Each time a call comes, the photo of his son appears on his cell phone, reminding him of his own father. This is how he pays his tribute to his father.'

'Very interesting, go on.'

'Abdul Kareem Sr was respected in society both as a teacher, which was his vocation, and as a religious scholar, which was his field of choice. He kept up a rhythm even when he died. He died at the age of fifty-one in 1951. Jaffer Sharief, my grandfather, was only fifteen years old then.'

'Why did he die so young?'

'He died of a burst appendix. A couple of months before, he had forced one of his friends to undergo surgery for the same ailment. But he was careless when he had the same problem. Apart from his son, Abdul Kareem, my great-great-grandfather, Abdul Lateef, had six daughters. After assuming charge as Minister of State for railways in the Union Council of Ministers, my grandfather visited his native village. Among the people who greeted him was a very elderly woman. She pulled his leg by formally introducing herself as his father's sister! She looked at the people gathered around my grandfather and recollected aloud:

'When you were a toddler, your pronunciation of certain words was funny. Once when I asked you where your father was, you replied—Chand is chasing Mukri. When I asked whom Mukri was, your mother Zehra told me, you meant *murgi* and that you call your friend, Fakru, Farku.'

'She was 102 then. Since then, Jaffer Sharief made it a point to visit her each time he went to his village. She lived to be hundred and six.

'Ma'am, I have information about the farthest link, to Abdul Usman as well. He had copied the Holy Quran in his own hand. We preserve the book as a family treasure.'

'Wonderful! Tell us what you know about your grandmothers as well.'

'My great-grandfather's wife was Zehra. She was on her deathbed when her son, Jaffer Sharief, wished to have her photo taken. But orthodox relatives stopped him saying that the patient might get frightened, assuming it to be a signal of her impending end. Jaffer Sharief immortalized her by naming his elder daughter after his mother. His mother-in-law was also called Zehra.'

'Two birds in one shot!' the backbencher commented.

'Shut up,' the teacher scolded him.

'An impressive commentary. Are there any other related incidents?' asked the teacher.

'Years passed. My grandfather was the Union Cabinet Minister of Railways then. A man of almost his age, called on him and said, "Jaffer, do you remember me? I was your Brahmin neighbour in Challakare. I stayed at your house when we were tiny tots because your mother wanted me to keep you company."

'Jaffer Sharief exclaimed, "What, Mrityunjaya!" He was swept away by waves of nostalgia and sat still looking at his pal for a few moments. He remembered the good old days. His friend used to have supper at the neighbouring Brahmin houses.

'Thereafter he would visit his friend's house and share childhood memories with him and his family over a cup of tea. One day Mrityunjaya asked, "Jaffer, do you remember our history master in the fourth class? He always asked you the same question—Jaffer, what was the name of the prince of Macedonia? And you would predictably say: Aleskander. The whole class would laugh and the master will prompt you: Say, Alek and then sander. You would parrot those two sounds correctly, but when asked to pronounce them together, you would again say: Aleskander!'

'When the Union Minister left the house, his friend and his family followed him to the gate. Sitting in the car parked on the roadside, Jaffer Sharief said, "Mrityunjaya, I was moved by your children's gesture when they touched my feet. I have imbibed this culture from you in my childhood without realizing the depth of its piety. I practised it with my mother and father before leaving for a long journey or returning from it. My children have learnt it spontaneously from me. Now their children involuntarily observe it. Certain guests have envied us for this great Indian tradition. It is disappearing even from Hindu families. I only wish that this courtesy can percolate to the succeeding generations".'

'Well done!' The teacher complimented the boy for such a detailed and dramatic a narration.

Then she turned to the class. 'My boys, you should keep the links with your past alive. You are the culmination of great and rich heritage. You have a duty to enrich and pass on the essence of your legacy for posterity. In the long line of heredity, we don't know its beginning or end at some point a particular figure will stand out, larger and brighter, illuminating the surroundings. For example...' she looked at the class quizzically.

They answered in chorus: 'Jaffer Sharief!'

'Ma'am, if we travel too far bachwards, won't we end up with a chimpanzee or gorilla?' asked the same mischievous voice from the backbench.

'Indeed, that is a certainty. You cannot help it. But, my dear friend, be careful that you do not end up with one such beast in your forward march!'

'How could we avoid that?' a worried voice from the middle row asked.

'That is the mission of our school!'

Shine, I have been repeating the names of Jaffer Sharief's ancestors and successors like a child practising multiplication tables. I fumbled every time.

Shade, who is Jaffer Sharief's hero?

Indira Gandhi, undoubtedly.

Any icon?

Perhaps, Tipu Sultan.

TIPU SULTAN

A GROUP OF CHILDREN were engaged in a bout of wrestling during interval in the school compound. Their shouting, howling, shooing, and clapping could be heard afar. After a couple of rounds, a new pair entered the ring. One was Jaffer Sharief. His opponent looked much stronger. Yet, he could not lift or turn the agile Jaffer, who deflected his every move. His grip was very firm. In one swift movement, Jaffer Sharief swept his opponent's legs off the ground, felled him on his back, and pinned him down to the ground, thus winning the game convincingly. Not allowing his rival to get up, he raised his clenched fist skywards in excitement. In that position his nostrils had expanded, eyes and mouth were wide open, the cheeks made two vertical brackets, the nerves of the neck projected out and a pit formed at the neck point. 'I am Tipu Sultan!' he yelled.

As a child Jaffer Sharief had been a staunch admirer of Tipu Sultan. He had played the role of that historic hero in the school play. At home, he climbed a mango tree in the courtyard, sat on a branch, as if astride a warhorse, brandishing an imaginary whip in one hand and a sword in the other like the sultan galloping towards the British.

Zehra Begum watched her son playing Tipu from a distance silently and with a smile.

Jaffer Sharief was in tenth class.

'My son, you were running high fever last night. Don't go to school today. I will send an application for leave through

Mrityunjaya,' Karim Sab said.

'Abba Jan, I must go.'

'But, you are very weak.'

'Does not matter. I don't want to miss the Kannada class.'

'Are you poor in Kannada?'

'Not so, but today our teacher is due to start a new lesson.'

'My child, listen to me, I will help you with the new lesson here.'

'Nothing doing! I want to learn the lesson in class. It is on Tipu Sultan.'

'So, that is the reason. You are crazy about Tipu. Okay, rest for a while. Don't walk to school. I will arrange a rickshaw for you. Now tell me, why do you admire the sultan so deeply?'

'For his valour, courage and self-esteem.'

'Not for his patriotism?'

'What is that?'

'The love for one's own motherland.'

'Indeed. But why did the sultan wage war against Bijapur and Malabar. Were they not parts of India?'

'During those days, India was a cluster of independent princely states. For Tipu Sultan, Mysore was his motherland.'

'Does that mean he did not fight and lay down his life for the freedom of India? He only was concerned about his province?'

'You are not entirely wrong. Yet Tipu is considered great for the rare courage he showed to resist foreign rule. Had he bowed his head before the British and brokered peace with them, he could have remained in power with all comforts, but with freedom curbed. He could not accept the very thought of a native becoming slave to an alien.'

'If every Indian thought the same, they could have easily thrown the colonial powers out long ago,' Jaffer Sharief remarked.

'Well that is the lesson to be learnt from the life of Tipu Sultan.'

'Perhaps we could have avoided partition too?'

'How does partition affect you?' Karim Sab asked, testing his son's sensibility.

'Had India and Pakistan remained one, what a powerful nation we would have been! Unfortunately that was not to be. What a tragedy! It divided the people by religion'—disappointment in the voice of Jaffer Sharief.

'You are right, but don't allow such thoughts to trouble you. Muslims were at the forefront when it came to shedding their blood for the liberation of India from colonial rule. Here the role of Tipu Sultan becomes all the more relevant. Hindus remember him as reverently as Muslims.'

'Abba Jan, did you believe that the Congress leaders, barring Gandhiji, were not unwilling to divide India along communal lines?'

'I didn't know that.'

'Could it be that India tactfully encouraged the evangelization of the northeast because religion would resist any possible advance by the irreligious China?'

'Jaffer, you take rest,' Karim Sab said and quietly withdrew from the scene.

Twenty-five years passed and Kareem and Zehra were no more. Jaffer Sharief won his first Parliament election. The spark of passion that he had felt for Tipu Sultan that had remained dormant began to rise. He floated an idea of holding a function to commemorate the warrior hero. The movement gained momentum. Simultaneously, he began to investigate if the sultan had any descendants. That did bear fruit. A direct progeny of the fifth generation of Tipu was located in Calcutta. He was requested to participate in the function.

A week before the meet, the celebrity guest arrived. He was over seventy years old. Jaffer Sharief observed the large, regal figure with awe and reverence. He held the guest's hand and kissed it. For a moment he felt that he was standing close to Tipu Sultan. He imagined the figure of Tipu as he had seen in paintings and searched for traces of his icon in the eyes, forehead, cheeks, chin and voice of his descendant. The guest sat majestically with his legs astride, chewing betel leaves and emitting a fragrance of cloves and cardamom. He spoke in chaste Urdu and laughed aloud moving his king-size tummy up and down. There was a miniature sword attached to a long thread tied around his neck.

After the celebrations, Jaffer Sharief gave the guest a ceremonial send off. Before leaving, the guest expressed a desire to shift his residence to Mysore provided he got back the landed properties of his ancestors appropriated by the government. An elated Jaffer Sharief gave an outright assurance.

Following the function, Jaffer Sharief left for Delhi to attend the three-month-long Parliament session. One afternoon, a week before Parliament ended, he saw a taxi halting before his flat. A group of children alighted followed by a woman in her early twenties. Jaffer Sharief kept his eyes at her charming figure. Then he saw a huge person slowly coming out of the vehicle with difficulty. Lo and behold, it was the sultan whom Jaffer Sharief had honoured recently. They trouped into the flat. The sultan hugged Jaffer Sharief. The woman was his fourth wife. They had got married recently. There were six children between the age group of two to twelve. The sultan had come to claim his properties.

Jaffer Sharief was surprised. But the guest had no confusion. The children occupied all available space. The sultan treated Jaffer Sharief as one of his subjects. He was out to encash the honour and goodwill that he had received from Jaffer Sharief.

However, Jaffer Sharief was convinced that there was not an iota of merit in the claim of property and that it was futile to follow it up. He did not say it in so many words. He pretended to enjoy the company of the children and their father. The sultan took particular care to insulate his bride from the unsolicited glances of others. After all it went without saying that Jaffer Sharief was a connoisseur of beauty.

To the consternation of Jaffer Sharief, on the third day of the sultan's arrival, another team of ten members arrived. They were a theatre group that had enacted a play on Tipu Sultan at a function held in Bangalore two months ago. They believed that just because they had acted in that drama, they had the right to walk into Jaffer Sharief's house. The team was on a sight-seeing trip to Delhi. Now the sultan and his family moved into a single room and the drama troupe occupied the drawing room, while Jaffer Sharief remained confined to his bedroom.

Jaffer Sharief wanted to run away from his flat. He booked a ticket for the next morning's flight to Bangalore. That night he hosted a dinner for the guests. The theatre group monopolized the conversation. Throughout the evening, each of them praised Jaffer Sharief and the new sultan. They dug out the history of Tipu and his equally renowned father, Hyder Ali. The valour and courage of Muslims were acknowledged with emphasis. At one stage, one of them drunkenly observed that Tipu should have converted all Mysoreans to Islam. The guests rightly guessed that the topic would please the sultan.

This eulogy touched the zenith of the sultan's pride and for a moment he forgot the need for restraint. He interrupted to narrate his experience with the legislator of Mysore during his stay there.

'Haji Seth is a great man. He was talking about Tipu Sultan. He was sad about the plight of the present Muslim community. He said that Hindus should be driven away from Mysore.'

While pronouncing the last sentence, the sultan's face glowed with hope and his eyes looked around for approval.

Suddenly a pall of gloom descended on the scene. An eerie silence prevailed. The theatre group, who were all Hindus, sat shell-shocked. Jaffer Sharief placed his hand on his head. He quietly retreated to his bedroom.

The sultan was clueless as to what had really happened. The others moved away one by one with their plates. But the sultan who was blissfully ignorant of the sensibility of others, picked up a chicken leg, looked at its size merrily and took a hearty bite. Later he unsheathed the sword hanging from his neck and with its tip started cleaning the divides of his teeth.

INTROSPECTION

'SHARIEF, YOU STILL KEEP awake?'

'Sleep evades me, Jaffer.'

'What is bothering you?'

'What else but you! For all your omissions, I bleed.'

'If so, then you must be relieved for all my successful commissions.'

'You forget the rules of the game. All virtuous deeds are credited to the account of Sharief.'

'Agreed, then Sharief must dutifully regret and repent and do penance, expiation, compensation and all such last rites.'

'Do you mean that my only duty is to suffer for all your lapses? I have independent functions.'

'Okay, what disturbs you now?'

'Young husbands end their lives; young widows are lured; young wives entertain paramours...'

'Enough, but what am I to do?'

'You must know them.'

'Don't tell me.'

'They are from your constituency.'

'I am helpless. I have not assured conjugal harmony to each couple in my election manifesto.'

'Imagine the pangs of rejection and separation.'

'Suicides often have causes and effects. One commits it to harass the other. It is an act that makes society look at the survivor with contempt. Cowards are the deceased. It does not need courage to die; it needs courage to live. And remember, love cannot be enforced.'

'Look at the devil in you. Yours is the language of an exploiter,' Sharief said.

'You may call me anything. I will call a spade a spade.'

'You are rationalizing your weakness.'

'Sharief, do you want me to wear the mask of a hypocrite?'

'Is it a confession?'

'No, an honest admission. Many appreciate me and they find solace in my presence,' said Jaffer.

'Lucifer wasn't without followers either,' Sharief added.

'What a simile! Remember, sin is the salt of life...' said Jaffer.

'...but don't forget, salt is white poison,' Sharief.

'You are exerting pressure tactics on me.'—Jaffer.

'We are two parallel lines; we will never meet. Let us keep a safe distance,' said Sharief.

'Modern theories claim that they meet at infinity,' Jaffer contradicted.

'You find an opportunity in every calamity'—Sharief.

'You are wise!'—Jaffer.

'You are anti-clock-wise!'—Sharief.

'While I was in power, I served my country, my region, my state, my district, my town and my village. Revenue to the exchequer, employment to the youth and foundation for future growth were my priorities. Yet, I am portrayed as partisan and corrupt.'

'Jaffer, you were supposed to be keeping a broad national perspective in the distribution of funds. Instead, you seemed to be driven by the ulterior motive of going down in the history of your state as a huge benefactor. I can hear the loud laughter of your king-size ego. You believe that posterity will sing paeans to you.'

'Sharief, you are right. The truth has started dawning on me. I am not sure that even the current generation would recognize me. I may have to cry out to prove my existence and relevance.

We are living in an age of collective amnesia. Yesterday is dead; tomorrow is unborn; what only matters is today.'

'Jaffer, finally you turn to Omar Khayyam. But what you have said was half-truth. In your beneficiaries' list, you left out the last two units. You should have honestly admitted that when you had power, you served your family and yourself too. The country generously offered you a chance to prosper and you grew. Not content with that, you wasted money, manpower and time for the benefit of none. Don't force me to substantiate with examples. You misused the comforts and facilities with careless abandon. For the state, you were virtually a white elephant. You were so power drunk that you twisted the arms of honesty to fall in line with rank corruption.'

'No genius is needed for the diversion of funds from one head to another. You are nothing in front of a farmer who sweats to produce food. You cooked his produce, served it to affluent and threw away the leftovers in dustbins while children starved on pavements.'

A hysteric Sharief was panting.

Jaffer remained shell-shocked.

'All said and done, Jaffer, I get disturbed seeing you gloomy. I prefer a cheerful sinner to a gloomy do-gooder. By the by, do you remember your first romantic adventure way back in your adolescence. You won the heart of a village girl by offering her a pair of semi-ripe bananas!'

Suddenly Jaffer regained his spirit.

'Hey, you are not being Sharief,' Jaffer protested. 'We better swap names.'

'Yes, in your view I am unlikely to be Sharief anymore. I am not joking. You have not forgotten that I have moved the court of justice against you. The lawsuit that I have filed is coming up for hearing next Friday. I will interrogate you myself. I will demolish you there.'

'One is revolting against oneself. This is a rare feat and a sign of growth and maturity. I am not at all upset. Rather I welcome it. It will help me come out clean. At the same time, I don't claim to be infallible. Sharief, be savage in your attack against me. Don't show any small mercy. No one else has the propriety and information to grill me in public. See you in the court.'

Observing the verbal duel, Shade whispered in Shine's ears—what a sporting spirit! Brave Jaffer is match for a noble Sharief. Jaffer and Sharief are setting an example of accountability.

Yes, Shade. It is not enough to be right. One should convince the world of one's righteousness. You are clean, but at times you will need to step in dirt and wash your feet publicly.

THE COURT

'YOUR HONOUR,' SHARIEF OPENED his argument, pointing an accusing finger at Jaffer standing in the box, 'here is a person who is dishonest to himself. He ditches those who love him, disowns those who stand by him, betrays those who brought him up, tortures those who serve him and takes the goodwill of well-wishers for granted.'

'Objection your honour,' Jaffer interrupted. 'Sharief is my alter ego. He claims that his voice is the voice of my inner self. For that reason, he takes liberty to critique and aim to strike a holier-than-thou posture in this court. To the best of my belief, I have been humane, just and dutiful. It is unfair to focus on my occasional skirmishes with my inner self. Sharief enjoys the fruits of my achievements, but keeps a distance from its means. He hunts with the hound and runs with the hare.'

'Argument incomplete. Objection overruled,' the judge announced.

'Thank you my lord! Now, may I be permitted to interrogate the defendant?'

'Please proceed.'

'Mr Jaffer, what is your most cherished principle in life?'

'Live and let live.'

'Make that clear.'

'Lead a life without, as far as possible, harming or hurting others.'

'This tentative statement indicates that you will not hesitate to do harm in certain pressing situations?'

'Who does not do so?'

'No counter questions; answer straight.'

'Yes, I repent that I have not given enough attention to my wife and children. Though I have been affectionate to them, I have failed in expressing my feelings for them adequately. I have given them room to suspect my absolute love for them.'

'For example?'

'Men in public life must necessarily move with the opposite sex. One cannot avoid communication with them. However, most housewives are susceptible to anxiety. Unfortunately, some of my rivals are mischievous. Often, I could not convince my life partner of my innocence. This must have affected her health even. On hindsight, I repent.'

'Does your wife distrust you?'

'I am not sure.'

'Your honour, may I be allowed to examine a witness?'

'Who is he?'

'Balan, before he passed away, was the conscience keeper of Jaffer.'

'Please proceed,' the judge, though shocked, allowed this.

'Balan! Balan! Can you hear me?' Sharief called out.

'Yeah,' Balan responded. His voice had an undertone of sorrow.

'How long has your association with Jaffer been?'

'From the days of our youth. Nay, perhaps since our previous births.'

'As a friend, how do you rate him?'

'Not undependable, not uncharitable, not indifferent too.'

'Balan, you are struggling to strike a positive note.'

'Oh no; my subconscious mind was playing truant. Don't be carried away by its sarcasm. He is lovable, concerned and kind.'

'I say that the person standing in the accused box is a compulsive and indiscreet client of sensuous pleasures, who hardly shows aesthetic preferences, and is immune to civic sensibilities and has little respect for the institutions of marriage and fidelity. Do you agree?'

'No, no, never!' It was a vehement denial from Balan.

'Jaffer has been unfairly misunderstood by onlookers. They do not know, or care to know, whether the frog in the pond drinks water or not. They take it for granted that it drinks. Indeed, he enjoys the proximity of the opposite sex. That, after all, is for biology to explain. Even his wife, who derives a certain sadistic kick by posing as a perpetual and perennial sceptic, believes in her heart of heart that he is incapable of breaking the diktats of ethics, not out of fear for his wife, but out of fear for an inner sense of righteousness,' he added.

'Balan,' Sharief asked, 'why do you vouch for Jaffer's innocence? He deserted you during your last sickly days on earth. Didn't he heinously display a sort of friendship amnesia?'

'I won't blame Jaffer on that count. I might have sinned my friends in my previous lives. I was suffering my own karma. Jaffer, even if he wanted to, could not have been different. He was only a tool in the hands of fate. May God bless him!'

Balan gasped for breath. 'Oh, here comes Babu. Here we spend time laughing uproariously and floating among the clouds. I may be spared. Babu will join you instead.'

'Babu,' Sharief called out in a choking voice. 'My son, can you hear me?'

'Yeah, Chand! I do hear you and continue to hear you. I always hear you!'

'Well, this is a court of self-introspection. Now, listen to me. I hold Jaffer squarely responsible for all that has happened. As a guardian, he might have been liberal, but not responsible; he might have been encouraging but not guiding; he might have been ambitious but not systematic; he might have been impatient, but indifferent too. Knowingly or unknowingly, was he not subjecting you to some sort of mental torture? Come on, this is an occasion for baring the pent-up emotions of your earthly existence. I have always been arguing for you. But as you know, Jaffer is more powerful than Sharief.'

'Oh, no,' said Babu addressing the judge. 'Forgive me for causing any misunderstanding. Nobody knew that I was punishing myself. I was a masochist. I threw away my life like an oversized dress. Life was too loose for me. I was ashamed to move on with it. I was his prime cause of worry. Enough is enough! I lie under the ground, waiting for him every Friday. We communicate with each other through our own language of silent prayers. I notice that Chand is growing old a bit too soon. His shoulder bones are sinking; his skin is loosening; his steps are slow. I notice white circles around his pupils; he needs help while climbing up. How deeply he loved me. He was pinning all hopes on me. I refused to rise up to his expectations. I chose haphazard routes. I was sympathetic to death. I used to fantasize about the presence of hungry death with its tongue licking its lips begging me for my life. It looked innocent. I wanted to pinch its cheeks, pat its head and hand over my life like a bar of chocolate. I avoided facing Chand. Yet, the sadist in me went on complaining that he stopped talking to me. I could not be of any help to him in his old days. The other day, when I saw his grandsons looking after him in his hospital bed, pressing, caressing and feeding him, I felt I missed this world of love and affection. I could only hand him lifelong agony. I knew that his heart was bleeding. However, he kept his calm, pretended to be courageous and served society. Sufferings, tension, stresses, strain, tears, cries...they comprise his daily bread.'

Slowly that voice faded into the thin air. Jaffer stood in the box with his head down and eyes closed. Sharief wiped his tears. Posting the hearing for the next Friday, the learned judge called it a day.

UNDER THAT BANYAN TREE

SHADE, DID YOU WATCH Sharief dissolving into Jaffer outside that courtroom?

I noticed. They have perfect understanding! Have you heard, dolphins swim and sleep at the same time. The left side of their brain sleeps for eight hours while the right side remains awake. Then the right side will sleep and left will swim. Each side performs complementary functions at the same time. Here Sharief observes principles and morality while Jaffer believes and indulges in practicability. While declaring solidarity and camaraderie with the Left, he has no qualms about accumulating wealth for the present and the future.

Oh, Shade, that is a sweeping simplification. No doubt, as an individual he loves his family and is concerned about their safety and well-being. That is a natural human instinct. It is a balancing act of nature. For each day, there is night, the moon waxes and wanes fortnight after fortnight. Exceptions, in the form of idealists, cannot be ruled out altogether, but in majority of such cases, their virtues are offset by inaction and incapacity. All are dolphins in one way or the other, as a rule.

I understand. A portion of the wealth so acquired by an adventurous person like Jaffer Sharief percolates directly or indirectly to society for its betterment. Jaffer Sharief, emboldened by the new confidence, ventured to adopt a whole colony of slum dwellers. It was another matter that he had to abandon that dream half way as it was much more than what he could gulp.

Such setbacks are not new in his career. In order to pep up the spirit of the Muslim community after the fall of Babri Masjid, he, even though a member of the government, agitated against the Prime Minister vociferously. He charged the Prime Minister with being hand in glove with the rioters to humiliate Muslims. Finally he renounced his power, faced the government's wrath, suffered ostracism, swallowed ignominy and was defeated in the election because of the machinations of his own party men. His lifeline passes through an undulating topography. Had he been an ordinary man, he would have become a nervous wreck by this time.

You are right.The world is mysterious and who we to judge are!

'No sirs, don't wash your hands off. You are the universal witnesses. If you turn away, whom will we, the lesser mortals, bank on?'

Ramu! How did you overhear us? Sure enough, we are the super witnesses. Yet, at times, we are also confused. Remember, truth is not ultimate, only approximate. Your truth need not necessarily be the truth of Jaffer Sharief.

For example?

You believed that he humiliated you by dismissing you from his office. But he maintains that you, even though you were his longest associate, did not care or bother to understand his dilemmas and compulsions. Who do we side with?

'Just because Jaffer Sharief sidelined an old acquaintance, no matter how massive his inputs were, he need not be branded unkind, partisan and irrational. But yet he rewards guys who were strangers to him and whose inputs are minimal, dismal or questionable. How would you rate him? Such eccentricity or angularity is an indicator of his concept of human relations,' Ramu remarked.

That means insensitivity to sincere service and lavish reward to sycophancy!

'In other words, those who work for Jaffer are well rewarded. He is generous. Sharief is miserly; he takes services for granted.'

Listen, Ramu, these are ex parte conclusions, which have no validity at the altar of the slippery ambiguous truth. What do you consider to be his positive traits?

'His sense of adaptability is awe-inspiring. He is comfortable with any age group—infant, child, adolescent, youth, middle aged, old, illiterate, highly literate, philosopher, artist, utilitarian, futilitarian ...you name a group and Jaffer Sharief is in it.'

Yah; I remember, Shade added. At one stage his close friends were a group of butchers and meat merchants in Shivajinagar. Of late, I've seen him courting singers of ghazals and qawalis and moving with world-renowned thoracic surgeons.

Ramu, how about sitting under that banyan tree for a while?

'Well, nothing like conversing under a banyan tree, with people of identical wavelengths on topics of common interests.'

While Shine and Shade played hide and seek around the banyan tree, Ramu relaxed casually on a portion of protruding roots of the tree, enjoying the murmur of its shivering leaves caressed by the gentle evening breeze.

The banyan tree is a guardian figure. Ramu, as was his habit, started talking into the air. It protects a world of beings under its far-flung branches. There are grasses, creepers, plants, bushes and shrubs; some medicinal and some poisonous; innocuous and obnoxious, some with prickly thorns and others with humble flowers; seasonal and perennial. This tree guards all of them against the vagaries of weather like torrential rain and the scorching sun.

Shade broke Ramu's soliloquy. It indeed protects the tiny ones but in the process make them dependent. It does not want them to grow taller.

'It shelters reptiles under its roots, insects inside its stem and birds on its branches,' Ramu said.

'And gleefully watches snakes gulping rats, woodpeckers picking worms and eagles catching doves,' Shine added.

'That is the law of nature,' Ramu exclaimed.

'Then, protection is also one such law. The banyan does not

deserve undue credit for it', Shine and Shade said together.

'All said and done, this giant banyan tree is the life saver of this village. It drinks up the toxic carbon dioxide and in return releases much needed oxygen for the survival of the surroundings...'

'Like?'

'Like Jaffer Sharief,' Ramu said simply.

'Substantiate your simile?' Shade asked.

'There is a world of parasites drawing nutrients from him. They include relatives, assistants, menials, managers, friends, priests, soothsayers, gossipmongers, Gandhians, professionals, journalists, air hostesses, brothel keepers...'

Ramu, please hold on. Is there anyone who exerts control over him?

'His wife.'

Is she powerful?

'She is the creator, protector and distributor. He owes all his prosperity to her prayers!'

Who then is responsible for his adversities?

'They are the reflections of her curses!'

Does he believe so?

'Indeed.'

'Don't you think it is a ploy to buy peace?' asked Shade.

'If so, it is not a bad bargain,' Shine added.

Ramu closed his eyes yielding to a siesta.

REJECTION, SEPARATION AND REUNION

'RAMU, COULD YOU DRAMATIZE your dismissal?' Shade asked.

'Friends, I have a fear. What are you engaged in—a study of Jaffer Sharief or Ramu?'

'Our attempts are to uncover him through whoever and whatever he came across. You have had a long association with him. And, you don't appear to be as fervent as the others to build a defence for him, unless it is called for.'

'Is that subtle flattery?'

'Never mind the colour of our statement. Lend us a helping hand in clearing the cobwebs of pretensions.'

'Okay, I shall oblige, come what may.'

He continued, 'It was the end of a twenty-year-long association. In 1992, he was the Railway Minister and I was one of his assistants. By that time, I was growing lazier and lazier. Maybe, in addition to my nature, Jaffer Sharief had no time or need as well for cerebral exercises. He decided to chip off deadwood in his office. That was understandable. But, the task of identifying the dispensable ones was given to a constable of railway police.'

'Constable?' asked Shine.'

'Rankwise he was an officer. However, in practice he was an apple polisher for whoever his boss was. Jaffer Sharief has a weakness for well-dressed and robust-bodied staff. That policeman was one of them. Once when he was escorting the minister, he looked at an approaching group of females with careful carelessness.

Suddenly, one of the girls screamed; another turned her face away; yet another giggled covering her lips. Our hero had forgotten to zip up his trousers and his fly was wide open. By the time he realized this and covered himself with a file, it was too late.'

'Later, I made fun of him saying, "for protecting your honour, your underwear deserves a Chakra award and that traitor, zip should be court-martialled." This joke did not amuse him the least.'

'Leave it and come to the topic,' Shade interrupted.

'The cop was not alone. It was a two-member task force. The other member was a heavy-headed female. She needs an introduction here. It is not out of place. It was a matter of sheer coincidence that while the constable suffered an embarrassment on his front, our female sustained a kick on her back.'

'That is interesting,' Shine said.

'She was waiting to meet the minister in the lobby of his residence chamber, along with many others. All of a sudden, she started jumping, turning and howling 'Oh my God!' Everyone went to her rescue but did not know what actually had happened. Then they spotted the culprit and burst into laughter.

'A couple of months before, a self-styled exorcist from Jalalabad had smuggled in a baby deer from the forest, outwitting the guards, and presented him to Jaffer Sharief. The bungalow had a sprawling courtyard and lawns where the little deer played and grew up. He was pampered by all. His favourite dish was beedi leaves, a habit that was the gift of the policemen who used to feed him with the leaves from the beedi rolls. Then he started sprouting horns on his forehead. Visitors touched and caressed him. Perhaps, the deer felt an itching sensation around the new horns. They were sharp. He often played with policemen by rubbing his horns over them.

'That day, nobody noticed the deer approaching the female from behind. In a single motion, he poked her abundantly inviting posterior with one of his pointed horns. Policemen came running, hauled him up and tied him to a pillar. But the damage had already taken place. The offended woman complained to the minister, who somehow pacified her ruffled feathers. But he marked the mischief. Before leaving, the angry damsel silently warned the deer of dire consequences.'

'Ramu, come to the point.'

'The constable and the woman called me to their office and asked what work I was doing then. I replied that I wrote love letters to girlfriends. Before walking out in a huff, I warned them never to probe a private secretary's job, since he was the conscience keeper of his boss and was not supposed to divulge his assignments. Unfortunately, Jaffer Sharief did not appreciate this principle.'

'Sair,' the constable began, moving his upper and lower lip up and down, 'these are the names which do not merit retention.'

'My name was at the top of the list. That was the day when Jaffer Sharief was to leave for Mecca on pilgrimage with his whole family. He looked at the list and decided to do a pious deed before embarking on the pilgrimage. He sent word for me. I had scented the plot. For some time he did not look at me. Then, he broke the silence: 'I say, I have decided to return you to your parent department.'

'There was a tiny overtone of contempt in his voice. He, in all probability thought that I would resist, argue or plead. He did not tell me why and I did not ask him why. Instead, I was brief: "Right, anything else Sir?" He said there was nothing else, so I thanked him and left.'

'A less loving thanks,' Shine commented.

'Quiet right. I came out of his chamber, reached my room, emptied a quarter bottle of army rum down my throat and recited from *Meghadootam* aloud:

> *kaschid kaanthaa virahagurunaa swaadhikaaraal pramattha*
> *saapenaasthamgamithamahimaa varshabhogyena bharthu*
> (Roughly meaning: for dereliction of duties, the boss suspended him, stripping him of all his powers for a long spell)

'After handing down the dismissal order, Jaffer Sharief opened the file on the deer. He called the chief of security staff and conveyed the order that the deer be transferred to his parent office. In this case, it was the Delhi Zoological Gardens! Thus, he had to make two sacrifices to propitiate the female and the policeman.

'Seven years went by and I always remembered him whenever I met my three brothers-in-law, who earned a decent livelihood from their catering business on railway platforms, which had been a gift from Jaffer Sharief. He must have been thinking about me writing communications when he wanted to vent his feelings to the Congress High Command in a distinct language. By that time, there was no love lost between him and the Party leadership.

'One day, when I was walking back from Bangalore Cantonment Railway Station after booking a ticket, a Fiat car stopped near me. I looked in and saw a smiling Jaffer Sharief! He had seen me from behind. He called me in, came to my house, saw my son and daughter, and shared a cup of tea. He fondly remembered the good old days of *idli* and *upma* he had eaten at my house. We acted as if there had been no yesterday.

'Briefly, this is the story of our rejection sans shock, separation devoid of pangs and reunion without thrill.'

'Ramu, you have been narrating events with measured candidness and struggling to steal undue limelight. Your attempt to equate yourself with him has not gone unnoticed.'

'Friends, there could be omissions, but I have been careful to avoid distortions. I have not attempted any intellectual summersaults.'

But remember, you are a child before him in stature, wisdom, vision, worldly experience, civility and culture. Agreed, he hurt your ego. But, you have no right to colour him to be less graceful. Distribution of favours may be unequal and injudicious. You deserve only that much.

'I am sorry, as a typical Homo sapiens I am not free from the inbuilt vice of ingratitude. However, my conscience reminds me that I owe him a lot for what I am today.'

Jaffer rejects, said Shade.

Sharief accepts, added Shine.

Although Ramu had bid them goodbye, he quietly followed them to eavesdrop.

Do you believe in Ramu's loyalty to Jaffer Sharief?

Loyalty, in its true sense, is synthesis and assimilation. There is no room for question, doubt or reconsideration. It is complete and abject surrender and total absence of ego. Loyalty does not always go with intelligence. Ramu, by his nature, cannot boast of such devotion. After all, he was groomed by Jaffer Sharief. Though he is a spokesman of loyalty, Jaffer Sharief is a practitioner of knowledge. Knowledge is the antidote to loyalty. Ramu follows the Jaffer Sharief-school. Knowledge, unlike loyalty, seeks analysis and deconstruction. It entails logic, argument, negation, contradiction, doubt and rejection.

Despite sharpening all his auditory nerves, Ramu could not comprehend the exchange of thoughts between Shine and Shade.

THE VILLAIN PHOTOGRAPH

SEVENTEEN YEARS AFTER THE dismissal:

'Sir, I am growing old.' There was an overtone of sadness in Ramu's words.

'That does not make news. It is but natural that metabolism slows down,' said Jaffer Sharief.

'I have not noticed it so far.'

'Don't you have a mirror in your house?'

'My mirror was cheating me and has been flattering.'

'Your wife doesn't stay with you?'

'She does not look at me.'

'She cannot be at fault. It is impossible to tolerate a maverick like you. Perhaps, you still write love letters to your girlfriends.'

'My eyesight is failing.'

'So, that is the reason, not because of the fear that I might dismiss you?'

'Dismissal is not an antidote to love. Moreover, I know for certain that love is the human emotion you love the most. You cannot play a spoilsport.'

'Tell me, how did the truth of aging dawn on you now?'

'I had a close-up photograph of my face taken. It was shocking to see wrinkles criss-crossing my cheeks, loose skin hanging around my neck, dark bags forming under my eyes and grey hair conquering my scalp.'

'You must reconcile with time. How does old age affect you?'

'As a lonely being, I feel insecure. I am afraid of tackling disabilities and diseases in the twilight of my life.'

'Go for a nurse. Shall I engage one?

'I am living hand to mouth, how can I afford a nurse?'

'Well, don't worry about that. So long as I am around, you will be taken care of.'

'And the nurse too, Sir?'

'She will be your headache.'

'I must thank you for your conditional assurance. But it does not give me adequate confidence. What I need is solid help.'

'I can guess what you are up to. You are a bully. You keep that up because I dismissed you from my personal establishment in 1992 and you lost the remainder of your service.'

Ramu laughed.

'Sir, you have disarmed me by preempting me of the chance to corner you. I feel like I am standing before a chess player.'

'Okay, let us play a game—argue your case. Tell me in what way I am responsible for the damage. Dismissing a member of staff was my prerogative. I used it to punish you.'

'No dispute. But, as a representative of the general public, I have seen you forgiving habitual offenders with a mere rap on their knuckles. I have been observing godliness in you on all such occasions. The punishment against me could have been conceived and executed with similar sympathy. What I mean is that the motive of punishment should be to reform the subject, not to wreak vengeance. Your order of dismissal was smacking of contempt against me which emboldened my parent office to harass me and drive me to the point of making me abandon my livelihood.'

'Ramu, you had no willingness to work; you were lazy; you were not taking up responsibilities.'

'Sir, you wanted a left-hander to function as a right-hander. Removing stains from a cloth is different from removing fat from the language. A word polisher will fail as a shoe polisher.'

'Leave it. But you were not the only one whom I dismissed.

What about your colleague?'

'Well, it was good that you asked this question. He too, had harrowing experience in the Intelligence Bureau. Unable to bear the harassment, he managed to secure a deputation to another office. But IB blocked his transfer. Hearing his problem, you intervened by personally talking to the then Home Minister and obtained his release.'

'You, too, could have sought my intervention.'

'One day I reached the gate of your house. Throughout, some negative current within me was pulling me in the opposite direction. Suddenly, your car passed me on its way out. I waved my hand, but you did not see.'

'That was not doomsday. What did you do on the following day?'

'I calculated your time of arrival and waited in the corridor of your office, hoping to bump into you. You arrived but proceeded to your chamber without raising your face. Though I wanted to talk to you, your staff maintained that you did not entertain visitors in those days. They knew that I had already fallen from grace. I had no courage or right to walk in.'

'You are an egoist.'

'I admit that. I have served only two masters in my life—one was the government of India and the other was Challakare Kareem Jaffer Sharief. Before the first, I had no qualms in displaying my ego, but before the second, I kept the wings of my ego clipped, though it used to ruffle its feathers sometimes behind your back.'

'Do you think I had not noticed that?'

'You had and I knew that you were waiting for a chance to humble me.'

'Can you substantiate your allegation that you were harassed in your parent office?'

'Here is an example. Among the Joint Secretaries who refused to accept me just because I was a reject, was one from Delhi. Before taking his decision he checked my antecedents. When I said that I was on the personal staff of Mr Jaffer Sharief, he lifted his phone to cross-check this and then virtually showed me the door. Later, I came to know that he had talked to your erstwhile secretary. They were brothers-in-law. The latter had some grudge against me because I was not siding with him in his cold war against you. Once, I had to tell him bluntly that I was loyal to the minister, not to him.'

'Why did you wait for seventeen years to rake up this issue?'

'I did not like to compromise my courage. But, today, I am weak, tired, less confident and alone.'

'Be specific.'

'During the first seven years I avoided seeing you. Then we had a chance meeting. After that I left for my village. Two years later, you called me to Bangalore and I worked in your office for about three years, hoping that since you were a Parliament Member, the government would pay my salary, but it did not. Then there was a two-year gap. Again you called me and I have been there for the last three years. The other day, you said I could pack up as you had no work. That provoked me to analyze the arithmetic of the past.'

'Ramu, do you mean to say that I could not dispense with an assistant whom I did not like.'

'I understand your predicament. Let me explain. In this case, my actions did not warrant a punishment. I was a victim. I had not committed any offence. Paradoxically, I was punished for refusing to commit a particular mistake. A personal assistant is not supposed to reveal to others as to what type of service he does for his boss. The female and the cop were pressing me to disclose exactly that. I do not blame them, they were executing, albeit thoughtlessly, your orders. In a nutshell, you punished me for not betraying you by revealing the subjects of your communications to dignitaries like the Prime Minister and the Party President. Your zodiac sign is Scorpio; a Scorpion commits suicide by stinging itself with its own tail.'

'Again, Ramu, you have not given me the alternate way to ease out unwanted baggage.'

'Yeah, I am coming to that. I am sure you knew the intricacy of this case. That was the reason why you did not give me a chance to explain. You avoided a discussion. Now, I will tell you how you could have dispensed with me without causing my heart to bleed. The Railway Board, which till the previous day was respectful, suddenly turned hostile after seeing your order. Even to obtain the relieving order, I had to plead with the clerk. I felt awkward even to face my family members.'

'Instead of a written order that I should be removed from your personal establishment and repatriated to my parent office at once, you could have shown the magnanimity of advising me, if not directly, to voluntarily opt out, stating some personal reasons.'

'What difference would that make?'

'Then my parent office would not have doubted me to be dishonest, incompetent or intemperate. A voluntary return would have earned some sympathy. Institutions are not deaf and blind. They display emotions common to individuals.'

'What motive do you attribute to me other than getting rid of a less useful assistant?'

'I had the false illusion that as a drafting hand, I was indispensable to you because you were a literate politician. You wanted to explode the myth of my importance. You intended to send a message to others that the axe could fall on anyone. You selected me for that model sacrifice.'

'But why?'

'Because the sadist in you wanted to see my heart bleeding.'

'Ramu, stop this nonsense. You are testing my patience. What is your damage?'

'You dismissed me in 1992. My date of retirement was 2004. I was an Under Secretary in 1992. Let us ignore promotion and pay commission during this twelve-year period. My bare salary ...'

'Put it in figures.'

'To be modest and conservative, easily 15,000 a month.'

'Fifteen into 144 or say 150; well over twenty lakh ...'

Jaffer Sharief calculated looking at the ceiling. The surface of his forehead was creased like a corrugated asbestos sheet. He asked Ramu to lift a briefcase from the floor. He slowly opened it and Ramu saw his right hand bringing out currency note. He held a hundred rupee note between his thumb and index finger.

'Come on, take it.

'What is it for, Sir?'

'Rush to the nearest photo studio and take a snap of your pretty face.'

'Why, Sir?'

'Look at the new print, I am sure you will find reflection of a ...'

'...of a?' Ramu was curious.

'Cunning fox.'

Ramu walked out in a huff.

Jaffer and Sharief indulged in a dialogue:

Did you read the face of Ramu? Sharief asked.

Frustration was writ large on it. But do you think his arguments hold water? Despite being offered chance after chance, he did not take them. Suddenly what has transpired? I doubt...

This guy witnessed gallons of milk being poured over illegitimate babies who do not even open their mouth, what is there to talk of crying! Ramu has not learnt the art of crying. A wolf can only howl; unlike a dog, it cannot bark. Ramu, a dog in a wolf's skin, cannot howl, only bark. He is shy, restless and withdrawn, Sharief remarked.

Do you approve the veracity of his claim? Jaffer asked.

It has a shade of logic. Maybe true, maynot be. He merits some benefit of doubt.

This fellow is rationalizing his greed. Sharief, you are too liberal.

Jaffer, we have seen manifestations of Himalayan greed shown by certain others. Compared to them, this is trivial. This plea at least has a semblance of reason. Accept or reject, but don't berate it.

Let us not quarrel over it. Goodnight.

Goodnight.

As the light was put off, a third voice broke the silence. It was a miserable attempt by someone trying to cry. It was coming from under the cot. But it did not awaken Jaffer Sharief, who fell asleep after consuming a high doze of Larpose.

GOD'S OWN VOICE

RAMU, IT IS A cloudy day, there's no activity. How about a trip down your memory lane? Asked Shade and Shine together.

Again you are deviating from Jaffer Sharief and focusing on me.

No harm, come on. Somewhere, sometime, you might touch a relevant cord that might unravel a new facet of his personality. We are not unduly obsessed with any particular subject.

Once I heard God's own voice in his words. That was over thirty-five years ago.

Good, the older the story the greater the nostalgia.

'Ramu, you are flying, with me to Bangalore tomorrow. I want you to cobble up a memorandum to the Chief Minister.'

That was my first ever experience of air travel. I was awestruck to see layers of white clouds floating below me. Immediately on arrival, I collected all points from Jaffer Sharief and started work. To my misery, my draft did not appeal to him. Revised, changed, modified, edited... all in vain. Each version produced wrinkles on his forehead. In fact, he had no points to add.

What was worrying him? asked Shade.

Maybe the form, Shine added.

Exactly. He fancied appearance, design and volume. He would be happier if a routine acknowledgement of receipt ran into several pages. He always opted for rooms larger than the normal size, the costliest food, the biggest car, heftier security personnel and taller personal staff. Once he went to a showroom and selected a typewriter with the longest cylinder. In those days only business establishments used triple carriage machines for preparing balance sheets.

Ramu, come to the point. What did you do with the report? Shine asked.

I was clueless. I meditated before the typewriter. Fed up, I tried an unconventional trick. This time I inserted the paper around the cylinder horizontally. When I finished typing, I pinned the sheets together and started going through the set. I did not notice that Jaffer Sharief who was passing through my room, was standing behind me and glancing at my new creation.

'Ramu, well done! It has now come out beautifully,' he appreciated my work unreservedly.

What he abhorred lengthwise fascinated him widthwise. It was a matter of preference of position. I laughed slyly.

After that mission was over, I decided to return to Delhi by train in order to save the difference between the airfare and train fare. But for no reason he made me miss my connecting train from Bangalore to Jolarpet, from where I could catch the Delhi bound train. He lent me his car to travel from Bangalore to Jolarpet but it had no petrol.

It was quarter to five in the evening when we left. His elder son, his brother and his brother-in-law joined me for a joy ride. It took half an hour to fill petrol and change the tyres. Jolarpet was normally a three-hour drive and we had two hours and forty-five minutes to get there. I, in the front seat, kept urging the driver to drive faster. The road was straight and vehicle-free. The car sped along at maximum speed. Before reaching Kolar, it started drizzling. We were approaching a hamlet. In the backseat, the young men were cracking jokes about anything and everything. There was a small curve ahead and the car suddenly skidded, moving towards some trees on the left. It looked as if we were about to crash against a huge tree. The driver was yelling for God but somehow managed to turn the steering wheel, and the car swerved and fell upside down into a canal of ankle-deep water.

Though shocked to the bone, we managed to come out, one by one, without even a scratch. The driver who had fainted by then regained consciousness soon. We abandoned our idea of proceeding to Jolarpet then and there. Seeing the accident, the villagers had gathered and were of immense help to us. With their help, the driver got the car moving and slowly, slowly, without headlights, we inched towards Bangalore. We reached Jaffer Sharief's house well past midnight. By that time, he had retired to his bedroom.

Next day, I heard Amina Bi shouting from inside. After some time, Jaffer Sharief came to the drawing room and informed me in a terse tone that I better leave. I nodded.

A week after I reached Delhi, Jaffer Sharief arrived. I was preparing to vacate the outhouse as he was visibly annoyed with me. Ready to receive the eviction order, I called on him. Contrary to what I thought, he showed unusual concern for me. He wanted to make sure that I had had no ill feelings for him. Incidentally, he mentioned that the cost to repair his car would be huge. Finally, he informed me that the memorandum presented by him had impressed the Chief Minister.

But, Ramu, where was the God's own voice?

Oh, I have deviated from the focus. Did I not tell you about the villagers? If they had not come, we would not have been able to take the car out of the canal. Again, they had to push it for a long distance before the engine started. Once it started, they came to the window expecting some cash, but we left without even saying thanks. Inside the car, Jaffer Sharief's brother lamented that if he had money, he would have given them few notes. That pinched my conscience. But, it was too late.

Next day, I realized that I was left with just enough cash for the train fare and food. I had paid for petrol and food the previous evening.

'Sir, could you spare me some cash?' I hesitantly asked Jaffer Sharief.

'No, I cannot,' he replied curtly.

Though his words hurt me, I vividly heard the voice of the Almighty, who was punishing me for my wilful omission of not paying the villagers the previous night.

Shine, forget the myth of divine intervention. What aspect of the attitude of Jaffer Sharief does this incident uncover?

Shade, it is obvious. He blows hot and cold. When the memorandum was to his satisfaction, he was all gratitude. Within hours, he had freed himself from that mental state and turned mechanical and business like.

ADVAITA

SHINE, JAFFER SHARIEF SWEARS by the name of secularism in every breath. Is it really out of conviction or by some compulsion?

It cannot be by compulsion. Under no circumstances can he adjust to fanaticism. Such is his nature. You too have been watching him. Can you visualize him otherwise?

No, I cannot. But, unfortunately, he has been mistaken by certain camps in either of the opposite groups. What is your opinion, Ramu?

I remember a funny incident. The former minister, Mohammed Ali, was the guardian angel of Jaffer Sharief in his early days as a Congress worker. Ali's doors were always open for Jaffer Sharief. By the time Jaffer Sharief rose to the level of a Union Minister, Mohammed Ali had almost retired from active politics.

'Jaffer Sharief, are you not a Mussalman?' Mohammed Ali's wife chided him. She could take liberties with him. That was the day when he, as Railway Minister, inaugurated a newly introduced passenger train from Kolar to Bangalore. He was having dinner at Ali's house.

'Why do you doubt it?'

'See the name that you have picked up for the new train, it begins with the word *suvar!*'

Pig is anathema for Islam.

The guests burst into laughter. First of all, she had not read beyond *suvar*. Secondly, she was ignorant of the Sanskrit word *suvarna*, meaning gold. The train was named *Suvarna Express*. Kolar is known for its gold mines.

Though this was a mock accusation, street Muslims generally thought that Jaffer Sharief was more a man of the Hindus than of Muslims. They resented that he moved around with Hindus, trusted Hindu friends more and was generous in helping Hindu religious causes. He believed in astrology, visited saffron clad holy men and according to some, had shown a feeble inclination to a Hindu orthodox group in his adolescence.

This was one side of the picture—Shade intervened—on the other, Jaffer Sharief was accused of fanaticism by certain members of the Hindu community. Their murmurs gained momentum when he started using his power for ensuring social justice in matters like recruitment. He was unperturbed because his conscience was clear. As a representative of the minority community he was morally bound to safeguard the interest of that section, as far as possible.

I shall tell you a personal experience, Ramu began. When in Delhi, Jaffer Sharief used to visit the dargah of the saint, Nizamuddin Aulia. On such trips, he would take me along with him. He would buy flowers in two cane baskets from the entrance—one for the saint and the other for the poet-philosopher, Amir Khusro. I would follow him, holding the flower baskets, wading through the swarming beggars for alms and prayer guides for commission. Covering his head with a towel, Jaffer Sharief would pray. I would stand outside, listening to the qawalis, waiting for his signal for flowers. Since it was a holy place, I also used to pray silently. This practice went on for quite long. Years passed. At one stage, I started receiving signs of inspiration to compose poems. That spell did not last long. Yet, I thanked, not Amir Khusro, whom I had not read, but Jaffer Sharief.

I had accompanied Jaffer Sharief to the sanctum sanctorum of the deity in Tirupati temple, circumventing the miles long queue. I had visited the Chidambaram temple as a companion to Jaffer Sharief. There one looks for the Lord, lying down on one's back on the rocky floor, with eyes fixed at the sky!

I remember another incident, Shine narrated. Jaffer Sharief on one of his frequent visits to the Shanakaracharya of Kanchi Kamakoti Peetha, lamented: 'I am disturbed and demoralized. Scandals and allegations chase me like wild dogs. Rumors malign me. Of late, I have started doubting myself.'

Swamiji replied: 'Politicians should rise to the level of sanyasins. Before entering this ashram, one renounces everything, including oneself. One does the last rites of oneself. One rejects even one's loincloth and enters into a new life of world service.'

'Politics is no less noble than sanyasa. A sanyasin has the alertness of a spy sneaking into the enemy camp and, at the same time, displays total detachment of an empty midnight market street. At that level, even if you rob the world of all its wealth, you don't rob of; even if you devour the entire food in the world, you don't eat; even if you kill all the living beings on earth, you don't kill. You are above all debilitating sensibilities in that state. Therefore, try…'

All of a sudden, they heard the call for prayer from a nearby mosque. Halting the dialogue, the acharya promptly offered a sheet to Jaffer Sharief and the latter performed the namaz in the meeting hall itself. This showed the strong secular mentality of Shankaracharya and Jaffer Sharief.

Ramu remembered one more incident.

'Sir, he looks like a fake character. We need not entertain him.'

I warned Jaffer Sharief against a visitor with a long beard, ash smeared all over the body, saffron robes and a rudraksha necklace.

'What should we do?' Jaffer Sharief asked.

'We will drive him away'

'Okay.' Jaffer Sharief turned the visitor away, but not before, stealthily stretching a clenched fist towards him. It contained a thousand rupee note! I noticed it from the corner of my eyes.

He gives; I share; that was the philosophy of Jaffer Sharief. The sharing would take different conventional forms of charity, alms, donations, subscriptions and help. But there was another form.

He would knowingly allow himself to be exploited by tricksters, swindlers, cheats, thieves, many of them being his own subjects. Here religion, region, caste and race had no bar.

Jaffer Sharief did not stop at it. He treated the honest and cheat alike. Shade explained this observation with a story.

A saint walking through a forest with his disciples was attacked by a group of thieves. They snatched away all their belongings and hit the old man with a club before they fled. He fell unconscious. His disciples sprinkled and splashed cold water on his face and he opened his unsteady eyelids. Just to test his condition, the disciples asked, 'Sir, can you recognize us?'

'Yes, yes, were you not the ones who beat me?'

You mean to say that Jaffer Sharief is on the way to sainthood?

Yeah, he is the victim and also the victor; he is the pain and he himself is the balm; he is the question and he alone is its answer! Shade said.

In a nutshell, he remains Jaffer and Sharief at the same time.

An ideal manifestation of the great Indian doctrine of Advaita, Ramu added.

CONCEPTS OF CHARITY AND BEAUTY

LOOK HERE, I AM waiting on the parapet. Come out, Shine called to Shadow.

Cool down, Jaffer Sharief is still in the bed. He is slightly indisposed. Come to the window, let us talk quietly, said Shade.

Is he concerned about his health?

Very much, at times bordering on hypochondria. He will not sleep alone at night fearing of any sudden discomfort. Often he mistook the upward movement of gas in the stomach for symptoms of heart attack. Doctors in the vicinity were regularly woken up at midnight. With much difficulty, they convinced him that it was gas and he was safe. Some of them even thought of shifting to distant localities. He kept close contact with physicians and specialists.

With nurses too?

Shut up, it is not time for cracking jokes, Shade admonished Shine.

Okay, but how come after being so alert, both his sons developed cirrhosis?

Any layman would attribute it to disorderly habits. But that would be an ignorant conclusion. In that group, all are not susceptible to ailments, as a rule.

Then what?

Inadequate or indifferent surveillance of wards by a non-resident father and a home confined mother, too, does not stand the scrutiny of science. We come across healthy bodies and disciplined minds among orphans too.

What do you think then?

Genetic engineering could possibly be the villain that catches the guardians off-guard and renders them disarmed. Way back, along the corridors of family lineage of either the male or the female, a certain ancestor would select an innocent descendent of a particular generation for gifting his ire in the gene.

Life has no rhyme or reason.

Yes, that is why Jaffer Sharief prays, prays and yet again prays!

He must be asking heaven why, of all the persons, he was chosen to bear the cross of misfortunes.

But he does not surrender to trials and tribulations. Instead, he faces them, survives them and hardens himself against adversities. This helps him understand and identify the helplessness of his fellow beings. He would not allow his left hand to know what help his right hand passes on to the needy. He believes that he is a trustee deputed to distribute the mercy of Almighty.

A true Gandhian! This attitude to life makes him taller than his contemporaries.

However, he is a soft target of exploitation.

Really?

His concept of charity has an element of mysticism. He credits all his losses caused by thieves, swindlers and cheats to the account of charity. He feels relieved when he realizes that he has been relieved of part of his wealth without his knowledge and consent. He may show mock protest or resentment for mere public consumption.

I remember a legend. A weaver of bamboo baskets would set out with ten baskets. He would place them in the courtyard of the first client and move away to the gate. However, the housewife would not agree on the price. At that stage, the weaver would ask her to throw back all his nine baskets. The greedy woman would do so, keeping one basket with her. She did not know that the weaver was practicing his daily charity. He would repeat this feat in the next house and the next until he has only one basket left. He would sell that and collect the cost for his livelihood.

Is Jaffer Sharief as mystic as that character?

No. But he is certainly the elder cousin of a typical traditional farmer from Kerala. The farmer stands under the jackfruit tree with sand in both his hands. His errand boy, up in the tree, drops the last fruit of the season from the tree. As the fruit falls the farmer throws the sand upwards, saying this prayer aloud:

One thousand for the thieves
One thousand for the beggars
Ten thousand for the owner

He thus invokes nature for a better crop next season.

This story visualizes Jaffer Sharief the charitable!

He maintained liberal and lenient relations with his fellow beings, Shine said.

Not always. Basically he is a utilitarian. He weighs the usefulness of others. Yesterday you fulfilled the assignment given to you with perfection. But, today, if he has no work for you, you are rejected. You were on the top of the world yesterday, but today you are an eyesore for him. In this world, people are of only two types—useful and useless. For him, price is more important than value.

You mean to say that Jaffer Sharief, knowingly or unknowingly, is a follower of Bentham's utilitarian principle of 'to be useful is to be beautiful'.

If I conclude that Jaffer handles beauty and Sharief charity, will you agree? Shine asked.

Such watertight divisions are not feasible, some overlapping could occur. Moreover, useless could turn out to be useful if retained for a period of seven years, they say. Similarly, one who was useful at one time, but rejected later for non-utility, could assume beauty at nostalgic moments. Yet again, beauty lies in the eyes of the beholder. One's usefulness need not necessarily be the usefulness of someone else.

Shade, we are totally confused. It is unethical to attribute motives or cast aspersions on either Jaffer or Sharief when the dividing lines are blurred.

Right. Let us reserve the judgment. They deserve benefit of doubt.

PROTOCOL

SHADE, OUR DESIRE WAS to treat this narration with a surreal tone, but...

Yes, I understand. Our vision is blurring halfway.

This happens when the subject is contemporary and colourful.

Jaffer Sharief is not a simple topic. One cannot read him. His thoughts, in their embryonic stage, sprouts in the forehead of mind and they reflect differently at the centre of the intellect. Finally, from the back of the brain, when they come out as decisions, they will be totally strange. It confuses even his confidants. They have no courage to proceed with any proposal. Vigilance, in the normal course pays; ironically enough, at times indifference also works.

That is cute!

Yeah. Ramu accompanied him on a tour. When returning to Delhi, Ramu typically left behind a suitcase containing the Minister's clothes in the state guesthouse at Agartala. He realized the blunder at the airport. If Jaffer Sharief would come to know of this lapse, Ramu would have been subjected to a dressing down in public. He kept mum for the time being. Boarding cards were collected and the departure of the aircraft was announced. Then Jaffer Sharief noticed a telephone in the VIP lounge and made a call to the Chief Minister which resulted in fixing a meeting between them within half an hour. The return trip was cancelled and the caravan returned to the guesthouse, much to the relief of Ramu. However, it was after some browbeating that he could recover the forgotten bag.

Why browbeating?

In the Communist-ruled state of Tripura, all government servants belong to the Party cadre. It was the same in the guesthouse. As a committed proletariat, it was the attendant's mandatory duty to harass all guests who appeared to be bourgeois or feudal. Thus, while sweeping the floor, he had hidden the luggage of the Congress Minister, by pushing it deep under the cot. Poor Ramu was ignorant of the nuances of such class hatred.

As Shade stopped, Shine added:

The message is clear—in the service of Jaffer Sharief carelessness is also helpful and uselessness is also useful!

Someone observed that if a diplomat says 'yes', it means 'can consider'. If he says, 'can consider' it means 'no'. And, if he says no, he is not a diplomat. Jaffer Sharief is a seasoned practitioner of diplomacy in political engineering.

You are right.If a matriculate seeks his help to join the IAS, he will say, 'can consider.'

Shine, the very reference to the IAS reminds me of one of his obsessions. His great wish was to have an IAS hand as his private secretary.

Shade, in the corridors of authority, officialdom must have harassed him in his younger days. Perhaps, he wanted to pay back his humiliation with interest.

One could not have helped but noticed a sudden change in him when he assumed power.

Yes, for a few days, he kept the lesser mortals, who were around him, at an arm's distance. He was going through the process of a VIP blossoming into a VVIP.

Stiff neck or stiff upper lip?

That was a canard spread by onlookers. First, they were unfamiliar with the basics of protocol. Second, they took it for granted that they were also shareholders in the new prosperity. Some of them had to weep before him to preempt rejection.

I remember an incident. After winning his third Parliament

election, he landed in Delhi with his family members. He had received sufficient hints of getting a ministerial berth in the Indira Gandhi government. He reached his flat, and his perplexed clerk, on seeing the master suddenly at the doorstep, out of sheer nervousness extended his palm to shake hands to congratulate him. That was an involuntary action. Jaffer Sharief is a man of unfailing courtesy. He obliged the clerk. But he marked the gesture as unbecoming of his employee's low status. As a result, the outcaste was put into quarantine for a few months.

But, can we blame Jaffer Sharief? Which boss could appreciate that action in the Indian context? As an adult, the clerk should have known his limits. A couple of years later, the clerk and his other colleagues lined up at the Delhi airport in the small hours of a December morning to see Jaffer Sharief off on his pilgrimage to Mecca. He moved down the line shaking hands as a gesture of gratitude for the send-off. Our clerk was standing towards the end of the queue. As the Minister approached, the clerk quietly withdrew from the line and hid under a lamppost. Jaffer Sharief watched his clerk's movements. He called him and commented while shaking hands with him:

'I knew that you would avoid me. I will not allow you to escape.'

Luckily, the next time Jaffer Sharief set out for the pilgrimage, the clerk was saved the ordeal as he had been dismissed from the Minister's service that afternoon.

Secondly, we are not sure that the so-called ostracism was for that blunder alone. Truth seldom moves in a straight line. Its trajectory is curvy, zigzag and nebulous. It defies common logic. It misleads witnesses. As Shine and Shade, we are mere observers from outside. We have no entry to the heart, brain and conscience of Jaffer Sharief.

I agree with your observation. He was taking time to acclimatize to the sudden change. Soon he regained his original disposition—pleasing, compassionate and reassuring. He carried each of his associates along with him and liberally distributed favours regardless of their uselessness and insincerity, even though the priorities appeared to be lopsided.

For example?

His personal staff, who were unknown to him till the other day, went berserk in appropriating undue benefits, one after the other, thus depriving his Party workers of due rewards, who were ready to die for him. The former group thrived at exploiting the generosity of Jaffer Sharief. His staff had prostituted the confidence that he reposed on them.

Did he not check this malady?

He strikes, but does not kill. If anyone died it was only because of his foolishness.

By the way, did anyone die?

A couple of casualties occurred. They were occupational hazards. But, before completing their last rites, the guys stage-managed perfect resurrection.

They outsmarted him?

He was helpless. He could remove the Chairman of the Railway Board who had equal standing as the Union Cabinet Secretary. But he failed to transfer a sweeper from his bungalow. The latter would emerge the next day, waving an overruling or stay order obtained from the appellate authority, Amina Bi.

For a brief spell, a relative took over as Jaffer Sharief's private secretary. Since he was an agricultural graduate, the minister was confused as to how to make use of him. Finally, he was made to water a coconut farm in an interior village in Karnataka. Soon, his political detractors purchased the private secretary and persuaded him to blackmail the minister. He was caught stealthily audio recording Jaffer Sharief's conversation with some visitor. Luckily he left voluntarily before he was dismissed.

The next secretary was an imposition by his political patrons. He was a shirker of the top order. In those days, at the instance of Jaffer Sharief, several cooks and drivers from the railways secured jobs in a Gulf country. Before leaving they called on the Minister to express their gratitude, and Jaffer Sharief commented in a lighter vein: 'Let my private secretary lead this delegation abroad.'

Despite these distractions, the even-tempered, merciful, philosophic Jaffer Sharief coolly enjoyed the drama with an element of detachment that is seldom observed in a consummate politician.

SCORPIO

WHILE SOME ACCEPT JAFFER, others welcome Sharief. Jaffer Sharief as a whole was also a subject of respect and ridicule, pity and pillory at different times.

Could you elucidate?

Indirect rejections are aplenty. For his declared loyalty, Indira Gandhi rewarded him with a junior berth in her government and allowed him a free hand to develop his home state. That was in 1980. After four years of an uninterrupted tenure in the railways, she immobilized him by installing Mr Ghani Khan Choudhury, an egoistic minister above him. The senior was notorious for his arrogance and effrontery. To give both the berths of one Ministry to members of the same community could not have been without a motive. An agitated Jaffer Sharief waged an open war against his senior, but without success. It was poetic justice. Sanjay Gandhi had used Jaffer Sharief, the junior Minister, in 1980 to harass the then senior Railway Minister, Mr Kamalapati Tripathi. However, Jaffer Sharief was freed from that uncomfortable task when Tripathi dropped out of the government and Sanjay Gandhi died in an aircrash. Perhaps, the sin boomeranged on Jaffer Sharief in 1984.

Nature maintains a cute rhythm. Hell and heaven are on the earth itself. You reap the harvest of your action in your own life, Shine commented.

In the general elections held immediately after the assassination of Indira Gandhi, Jaffer Sharief defeated the firebrand socialist,

George Fernandez. Buoyed by this euphoria, he was confident that no Prime Minister could ignore him. But he had no place in the Rajiv Gandhi government. That was a rude shock. However, the same Rajiv Gandhi rehabilitated him towards the fag end of his government's tenure. He inducted Jaffer Sharief in his council of ministers as a junior minister for coal. There, too, Jaffer Sharief couldn't get along smoothly with his senior colleague, Mr Vasanth Sathe. That spell lasted for one and half years.

In the elections held immediately after the assassination of Rajiv Gandhi, the Congress formed the government under the prime ministership of P.V. Narasimha Rao. That was in 1991. Rao had little more than an average understanding of Jaffer Sharief, but he chose him to head the all important railway ministry. As the Cabinet Minister of Railways, he was amongst the hierarchy of VVIPs, next only to the Prime Minister, the Home Minister, the Finance Minister, the External Affairs Minister and perhaps the Defence Minister. Among one hundred crore Indians, Challakare Kareem Jaffer Sharief thus became the fifth most important person in the country.

Narasimha Rao allowed Jaffer Sharief the freedom he had never enjoyed under any other prime minister. This helped him lay the foundation for the future growth of Indian railways.

Then the tragedy of the demolition of Babri Masjid took place. Jaffer Sharief held Narasimha Rao responsible for not protecting the monument. He openly revolted against Rao and announced publicly that if the need arose he could pull down the government for that lapse. This emotional outburst resulted in the loss of the coveted railway portfolio. What was more, Jaffer Sharief was reduced to a Minister without portfolio. When he landed at the Delhi airport after a heart surgery at London, he was prevented from entering the office of the Railway Minister. That direction was delivered at the airport by a special messenger of Prime Minister. The revenge did not end there. Narasimha Rao denied him ticket in the subsequent Parliament election. Had he contested he would have won with thumping majority.

Here Shadow intervenes:

Let us look at these developments from a different angle. Those who tortured Jaffer Sharief were ultimately paid by the same coin. Ghani Khan Choudhury and Narasimha Rao had to eat humble pie. Choudhury, though inducted to a trivial portfolio, was shunted out unceremoniously. Rao, too, had to swallow ignominy. That former Prime Minister was denied a ticket to contest for Parliament by the Party President.

Strange are the ways of the rise and fall in public life, Shine commented.

Jaffer Sharief was the foremost among the first few who had advocated the entry of a reluctant Sonia Gandhi into politics by taking over the reins of Congress. Later, he thoughtfully avoided joining the sycophants clamouring for Sonia Gandhi to head the Government of India. While Jaffer Sharief was not rewarded for the first, he was awarded a painful punishment of isolation for the second!

It is the reverse rhythm of nature!

Isn't his zodiac sign Scorpio? Shine asked.

Why?

In certain conditions, scorpions go mad and sting themselves with their own poisonous tails and commit suicide, Shine added.

A cursory glance through his career will reveal that he is not a quintessential Scorpio. Certain scorpions are the deadliest on the land. An explorer chased by an elephant, hid inside a narrow cave in an African jungle. As the tusker pushed his trunk inside, it hit into a scorpion that stung it. The elephant retreated in acute pain. After four or five hours, the man emerged and saw it lying dead. When he just pressed its belly with his foot, his shoe sank into the carcass of the pachyderm that had turned into pulp. The story does not end here. After a few weeks, the explorer noticed a black spot beneath his toe. Doctors diagnosed it as some infection. Actually, the venom from the body of the elephant had penetrated the sole of his shoe and then entered the skin. To be brief, he had to have his leg amputated to stop gangrene from spreading, Shade said.

But Jaffer Sharief is not revengeful or violent even against his worst detractors, Shine said.

Yes, he is forgiving by nature because he has observed and studied the world more closely than many of his fellow travelers. Sometimes Jaffer Sharief exhibits the character of the birth sign of Cancer. A crab on the narrow bunds of paddy fields confuses the onlooker by the way it moves—forward, backward, right or left, unpredictable—Shade commented.

Yes, Jaffer Sharief is a combination of Scorpio and Cancer, said Shine.

In other words, less of Jaffer and more of Sharief! Shade concluded.

INTERVIEW

'SIR, WHAT IS YOUR favourite pastime?'

'Chatting with friends and listening music. The former is frequent; the latter is few and far between. I spend hours sitting with journalists and politicians, but I forget myself in the company of small-time associates like certain petty merchants of Shivajinagar of my younger days. I attend concerts of ghazals and qawalis, but get emotional when I hear someone humming those lullabies my mother used to sing while swinging the cradle of my young siblings. I used to babysit for my sisters and brother.'

'Do you remember crying for something when you were a child?

'Yes, for a wooden toy, for a bigger share of sweets and for an animal story. Once after winding the string around a top and flinging it against the ground, it did not spin because I lacked the skill. That day I cried. Being the eldest son, my parents pampered me. But I did not become wayward, thanks to my guardians who knew how to bring up children.'

'What brought you the greatest pleasure?'

'Nothing like lying on a wide bed in dim light playing with my young grandchildren. They kicked, shoved, pushed, pulled and rolled over me. They teased and made fun of me, disrobing me of all my vanities and snobbishness. I hate children growing up. Innocence is the price they pay for growth.'

'What is your constant fear?'

'Old age and indisposition, both of myself and my dependents. I feel secure in the company of doctors. I am uncomfortable when I have to sleep alone in a room, it's a sort of phobia.'

'What do you hate the most?'

'Of being the object of indifference.'

'Yes, we have noticed that. While presenting the Railway Budget, you completely claimed the limelight. Yet, two days later, on the eve of presentation of General Budget, you look for a seat closer to the Finance Minister.'

'I don't deny that.'

'Do you think you're good as a negotiator or arbitrator?'

'I have intervened to bring about peace in certain families. Some cases have been successful, others not. Of late, I realize that each family is a battlefield, either of hate or of love, indifference, disrespect, suspicion, possessiveness, jealousy and the like.

'What is your opinion about marriage?'

'The so-called union of hearts is a myth. If a couple can work out a common minimum programme and adhere to it, well that is enough. But, ego is the villain. Willingness to sacrifice could save the boat from sinking. All said and done, shorn of verbiage, it boils down to the truth that women's ways are inscrutable.'

'That is a male chauvinistic view.'

'Maybe.'

'What is your greatest temptation?'

'Food. Once I was a voracious eater. These days I control my diet. Though Amina Bi loves me selflessly, my second wife takes care of my day-to-day chores more carefully.'

'Who is she, Sir?' The interviewer was taken aback.

'Diabetes.'

'How?'

'She reminds me as to what to do and what not to do. She catches my hand if I long for sweet, salt and fat. However, I don't heed her advice of an early morning walk and a pure vegetarian diet. I have a weakness for one thing and I will try to pick it up even from my neighbour's plate.'

'What is that?'

'I look for black mustard seeds, green curry leaves and red chilly pieces on the top of semi-solid uppuma, made of milky white *rava*. The chilly pieces turn violet after frying. They entice me with their mischievous pungent aroma.'

'You are a keen observer of colours. Perhaps that is also a reason for selecting daughters-in-law from Kashmir?'

'That was not because of their skin-colour. Kashmiris by nature can withstand great sufferings and we are good at offering various types to them.'

Jaffer Sharief looked at his watch and signalled to the interviewer to wind up.

'Sir, one last question.'

'Who is your favourite heroine?'

While moving towards the door, Jaffer Sharief, at his humorous best, announced to the amusement of the camera crew, 'Amina Bi.'

The TV channel team packed their equipment and went out of the room. As they stepped down to the car porch they saw him entering his car. The media girl, showing mock hesitation, approached him. He lowered the windowpane.

'Sir, one for the road?'

He laughed. She had won him by her disarming smile.

'What do you want to know?'

'Any grief-stricken memory from your childhood?'

He sat still pensively for a moment and asked her, 'Where are you going?'

'My studio, at Frazer Town?'

'Get in, I will drop you. On the way I will try to recollect.'

She jumped into the car and opened her notepad.

'I was nine years old,' Jaffer Sharief began. 'One morning, I saw a baby squirrel lying in the courtyard. Perhaps, it had fallen from its nest. It could hardly open its eyes. I carried it carefully and ran home. It looked very cute. My mother initially discouraged me but when I grew recalcitrant, she allowed me to keep it as my pet. I named him Kittu. It grew day by day. I fed him with grains and fruits. Kittu ate from my palm. I used to sit watching his quick moving lips, glowing eyes, panting stomach and swinging silken tail. He would crawl over my feet, climb up my legs, run around my chest, rest on my shoulders and dive into my shirt's pocket. Kittu responded to my calls by a typical sound. One day, few drops of cold water fell on his back from my hand. An annoyed Kittu, beating the ground with his tail, scolded me in anger *chil chil chil chil chil*. My mother came running, picked him up, dried and consoled him.'

'My friend Mrityunjaya was visiting me. When he saw the squirrel coming out of my pocket suddenly, he was wonder struck. He could not believe that I had tamed a squirrel. He yearned to touch it, but had no courage. Kittu used to bite with his chisel-like teeth. I stood before my friend, caressing the three long stripes on his back. Mrityunjaya told the story about the origin of those lines. Lord Rama's monkey brigade was erecting the bund with rock, wood and mud across the southern strait to cross over to Lanka, when a squirrel joined them. It plunged into the sea first, swam out to the shore, rolled over on the beach and then when its body dried, it shook its limbs, scattering the sand over the bridge. Rama observed its selfless service and was immensely pleased. He ran his merciful hand over its back and ever since, squirrels bear the imprints of the fingers of the Lord.' Mrityunjaya honoured Kittu by folding his hands at him.

'Kittu used to play with me in my bed till midnight. I had made a cradle for him. I used to tell stories to him. He would wait for me to return from school. I used to forget my homework those days.'

'One day a tribal palmist woman appeared in our courtyard. My mother offered her alms. She looked at my face and prophesied that I would one day rule the land. My mother was very happy. Suddenly Kittu climbed over me. Watching this, the tribal woman warned my mother that squirrels are children very dear to God. If a squirrel dies in our custody, we would have to offer gold equal to its weight to God.

'I said, "my Kittu is safe with me".'

'Then came Id. In the afternoon, I fired a long string of crackers. Its explosion lasted for a few seconds. I did not foresee that the sound would frighten Kittu mortally. He jumped and ran away into the compound and disappeared. I called him repeatedly. Finally, he returned very dispirited. He did not move. That night he didn't eat. He was groaning in pain. I did not know what to do. I could not sleep. Next morning, I saw him lying still. After some time, he started moving slowly. But he was really ill. Somehow, he came out of the house, and slowly climbed up the tree in the courtyard. From there he did not return. I looked for him, but could not locate him. He was not crying. By afternoon I became restless. I did not move away from the foot of the tree. Then, as if to give me a last glimpse of him, he appeared on a branch. He was hanging across it. I called "Kittu", but he did not respond. But he kept on looking at me without blinking. We remained looking at each other helplessly. I thought that he would return by evening. I left and when I went back to that spot, Kittu was not there. I thought that he was able to move, but he did not return.'

'Next morning, I was determined to locate him. He was not in the tree. I searched everywhere. Finally I found him. I saw him hanging over the adjacent telephone post, across a wire. He was dead. His fur was moving in the air. His tail and head were touching each other. Seeing him lifeless I became numb. My mother was also restless about Kittu. I concealed the truth from her. His body remained on the post till it decayed and dried up. I used to watch his body without my mother noticing. But, later I came to know that mother was fooling me as I was fooling her. She had seen the body of Kittu the very first day. For a few days, I used to weep alone pining for Kittu. Whenever, I saw a squirrel I took it for my Kittu. Slowly I negotiated that grief. Such are the ways of the world!'

Jaffer Sharief took a long breath. He added: 'I suffered a greater loss later in my life. That took place in the first month of the last year of the last century. I will tell you about that some other day. We've reached your studio.'

The girl had forgotten time and place. She was so absorbed in the grief. While getting down, her eyes were moist.

Shade, we should not miss the description of the 'greater loss'.

Yes, let us keep track.

TRAGEDY

THE TWENTY-NINTH DAY OF January of 1999 was quite like any other day at the residence of Jaffer Sharief. Normally the family members were very late risers. That being Friday, they were all very relaxed. Khader Nawas Sharief had returned on Thursday night after a three-day visit to Katpadi. Those days, the son used to avoid coming face to face with his father. Jaffer Sharief, therefore, was not aware that Babu, as his second son was called, had come back from a tour.

A wail from Babu's room woke everyone, including his parents. His wife was crying and calling others. Babu was lying on the bed motionless. She tried to awaken him but to no avail. She feared the worst and soon realized that she was right—Babu was dead! His body had become cold.

It was cardiac failure. Babu had nephritic complaints too. In his teens he was lean and tall with curly hair. By nature he was intelligent and humorous. He grew obese in his early twenties. He was the only child who had inherited his father's leadership traits. Jaffer Sharief was pinning his hopes on him. He had his own followers and well-wishers who were ready to stand between him and death. But, death outwitted all of them. It snatched his last breath and ran away while he was asleep.

The house was filled with mourners. The road in front of the house became an ocean of humans. People watched a crestfallen Jaffer Sharief sobbing for the first time, that too, inconsolably. He held whoever came close to him tightly as though he had become an orphan. Wailings reverberated through the house.

The funeral procession was miles long. Babu had built up an identity independent of his father. Burial and related rituals were over by evening. Jaffer Sharief, who had to follow his son's body on his last journey, had not taken even a drop of water. He was acutely diabetic.

'Sir, you have to take little food,' his doctor pressed him.

'Do I have to?' His voice was hardly audible.

'Yes, you have to.'

He looked at his wife, helplessly. Tears had dried in her eyes. Jaffer Sharief sadly asked whoever reached before him, 'Where is my Babu?'

That night, a couple visited the devastated Jaffer Sharief. They stood before him and Amina Bi. Jaffer Sharief lifted his swollen eyelids up. The man held Jaffer Sharief's hand and caressing his palm asked: 'Do you remember us?'

Jaffer Sharief shook his head.

'We are meeting after seventeen years. Babu was my son's bosom friend. They were college students then. My son joined Babu in Delhi for that year's vacation. He was staying in your bungalow. He used to call us and tell us about the exciting days with his friend. Then came a call that was not from my son. It was a message that my son had an accident and was hospitalized. When we reached, my son was in the ICU.

'They were playing on the lawns of your bungalow, practising high jump. In one attempt, my son fell and hit his head against the hard ground. His neck bone was broken.'

'Kaliya was your son,' Jaffer Sharief recollected.

'On the third day of our arrival, Kaliya breathed his last. A few moments before his death, he asked me, "Daddy, will I survive?"'

'My son, Babu, almost went mad on the day of Kaliya's death. I had to instruct my security staff to keep an eye on him lest he turn violent and commit any mistake,' Jaffer Sharief remembered those days.

'He made the mistake after seventeen years,' an onlooker, who believed that the premature death was due to carelessness, whispered in the ears of his companion.

'We absorbed the grief. We hope our presence will help you overcome the shock,' Kaliya's father said before they left. For the first time, Jaffer Sharief stood up to see them off. He then helped Amina Bi to return to life by forcing her to take a few drops of tea.

Grief could be tackled by grief alone.

A couple of months later, Sonia Gandhi came down to Bangalore. She visited Jaffer Sharief at his house and consoled him, his wife and Babu's wife before she returned to Delhi.

By then, eight years had passed after the tragic death of her husband, Rajiv Gandhi!

Jaffer Sharief received a condolence message from the President of India, Mr S.D. Sharma, whose son and daughter-in-law had been shot dead fifteen years ago.

Death is Almighty! It accompanies one throughout one's life. It moves with you, sits with you, sleeps with you, joins you in all your journeys, partakes of the food and carries you with it finally!

Amina Bi and Jaffer Sharief limped back to normal life very slowly. They started tasting spicy pickles; they started watching movies on TV and they started planning the remodelling of their sitting room. One day, when Jaffer Sharief opened a book from Babu's collection, some sheets of paper fell down. They were the scribbling of Babu. He was bidding farewell to his people in few words. Perhaps, he knew that he was inching towards his end. At one point, he addressed his father, 'Chand, think of me at my best. Be cheerful. Whenever I appear in your thoughts, remember an incident that I narrate here. This will lighten your mood.'

Babu pens it down in the third person.

POLYGAMY

COME SHADE, SOMEONE IS reading the note left behind by Babu. Let us listen, Shine said.

Well, the narration is interesting, Shade added.

It began with an explosion:

'I won't allow your friend to step into my house,' Amina Bi warned Jaffer Sharief sternly.

'Who you are talking about?'

'Who else but that pal of yours from Whitefield!'

'Oh! Leader! What happened?'

'You don't know? Did he not tell you?'

'Why don't you tell me?'

'I detest pronouncing his name. He is going to rope in another female, *thu, thoo*!'

'Poor fellow, he is helpless.'

'Don't try to be smart with me.'

'That is the wish of his mother. She threatens to commit suicide if he does not oblige.'

'Bullshit! No mother worth her name will entertain such a wish. He is a rogue. He twists the arm of that old village woman.

'His first wife does not object,' Jaffer Sharief said.

'That bully is intimidating her. Let me ask you. Why do you shield him so indulgently? I know you. I doubt your intentions as well.'

'What do you mean?' Jaffer Sharief asked.

'Who knows! You may also follow suit!'

'Shut up! It is his personal matter. Can I meddle with it?'

'As a so-called friend, you have a moral duty to prevent him. Have you, at least, made an attempt to dissuade him?'

'No, I have not.'

'There you are. It is tantamount to abetment.'

'How could I convince you of my innocence?'

'First of all, you are not innocent. If you are, then sever all friendship with that lecher.'

'Listen, he is the member of Parliament of my neighbouring constituency. I have a public life.'

'Is it that men of public need not have respect for morality? To err knowingly is a sin in itself, but to recognize it, is a greater sin.'

'Are you calling me a sinner?'

'Don't ask me, ask your conscience.'

'My past, so far, is an open book.'

'You believe that I, being unlettered, cannot read a moth-eaten, weather-beaten Jaffer Sharief!'

'This argument will not take us anywhere. That boy will get upset,' Jaffer Sharief pointed at Babu, who was enjoying this fight.

'I seek solace in children,' Amina Bi wiped her tears, looking at Babu.

'Ammi Jan!' Babu, fresh from the naughtiness of college life, intervened. 'Men are of three types: bachelors, husbands and widowers. Once he married you, he ceased to be a bachelor. So long as you are around and kicking, he cannot be a widower. Now, the only course left to you is to make him a model husband.'

Amina Bi laughed and added: 'To mould an ordinary husband out of your father I need a hammer and chisel.'

'Remember Ammi Jan there are three kinds of husbands: prizes, surprises and consolation prizes.'

'Will you shut up, Babu?' Jaffer Sharief interrupted.

'Don't stop him, he is intelligent, he is my son,' Amina Bi replied.

'Okay agreed. To escape from this mess, I will take you to a movie; get ready,' Jaffer Sharief tried to pacify his wife.

'I have not forgotten my horrendous experience last time. After the show, you bumped into some of your party workers and sped away with them, forgetting me. I was calling you from behind but you did not hear me. I stood helpless. Luckily, a couple in our street happened to see me stranded. They helped me reach home.'

'Don't harp on that incident again and again. I was absent-minded then. Moreover, you should have kept an eye on me and prevented me from leaving you,' Jaffer Sharief winked at Babu.

'I will have to order a pair of glasses to keep track of you.'

'Order magnifying glasses and, if need be, a pair of binoculars.'

'Mummy, you need a periscope as well.'

'What is that?' Jaffer Sharief asked Babu.

'With a periscope you cannot escape surveillance from any difficult and awkward angle.'

'My God! I am surrounded by spies,' Jaffer Sharief said in mock horror.

'Still you wriggle out!'Amina Bi added.

As Amina Bi went inside to get ready for the theatre, Babu went closer to Jaffer Sharief and whispered in his ears: 'Chand, do you know, I am also a spy!'

'Really?'

'Yeah, that is how I arrange for my pocket money.'

'You brute!'

'Don't worry, I will take care of your interest too—not free but at a premium.'

Jaffer Sharief laughed aloud.

Babu ended the note with an 'adieu' in red ink.

Babu has visualized Amina Bi to be a powerful character, Shade said.

She indeed is, Shine added.

Did they go to the matinee?

Yes, I vividly remember it. That was also a funny incident.

MATINEE

'ENOUGH OF IT! LET us go,' Amina Bi said inside the theatre.

'What happened? The picture is only half way through,' Jaffer Sharief asked.

'I don't like it.'

'But why?'

'The story is immoral, absurd and disgusting.'

'It's mere imagination, I'd say.'

'Yes, imagination pollutes the mind. You may enjoy the theme of extramarital relations, cheating and infidelity, but I do not.'

'Then close your eyes.'

'No, my seeing is not the issue here. I want to protect you from viewing it; um, get up.'

Jaffer Sharief reluctantly obliged. They moved to the door, groping in the dark, without an usher, and then reached the lobby.

'Sir, what happened?' The theatre manager asked.

'She did not like the story and dialogue.'

'Madam,' he turned to Amina Bi, 'this film has a message.'

'What is that?' Amina Bi sounded sceptical.

'Indifference kills love. If the partner flirts with a member of the opposite sex, even under the very nose of the spouse, it has no effect. That is indifference. That is the death of love,' the manager parroted a review that appeared in the press.

'Among the viewers, how many look for the message?' She walked out holding Jaffer Sharief's hand.

They entered a restaurant. Amina Bi was clear about what she wanted: *dahi vada*. Jaffer Sharief went on shuffling the items in the kitchen of his mind and opted for *rava idli*. The waiter served them. While Amina Bi enjoyed her snack, Jaffer Sharief glanced at the next table and lamented: 'I should have ordered *kara bath*, it's spicy.'

'Learn to live with what you selected. Man is a hopeless tribe!'Amina Bi frowned at him.

On the way back home, they got stuck in a traffic jam.

'Trrrrrrr Naka, Trrrrrrr Naka, dan ... dan....dan,

Trrrrrrr Naka'

A procession was passing through.

They watched from the car. It was a funeral procession accompanied by drummers and dancers. An elderly man was being taken for cremation in a carriage. The body was in an erect sitting position with garlands and makeup. He was wearing glasses and looked as if he was smiling. Jaffer Sharief looked at the face. He felt like the corpse advising him: 'Look, young man, how respectful I am even in death! In fact, I am not dead. The real death is indifference. Many claim to be alive but are already dead.'

At home, Jaffer Sharief congratulated himself in silence: 'Fortunately, Amina Bi is not indifferent to me. She believes that I am still useful in the house. Thank God!'

WEDDING ANNIVERSARY

JAFFER SHARIEF AND FAMILY had just returned after attending a neighbour's wedding anniversary.

'We too must celebrate our wedding anniversary,' Babu said.

'Our wedding?' Munna asked.

'Daddy's wedding,' Baby corrected.

'Daddy's alone?' Munni queried.

'Okay, the wedding of Amina Bi with Jaffer Sharief,' Baby clarified.

'Ammi Jan, what is that date?'

'Who knows?'Amina Bi said.

'Chand, do you know?'

'I don't remember,' Jaffer Sharief faked ignorance.

'We will find it; tell us the year,' Munna said.

'It was in 1957,' said Jaffer Sharief.

'Month?'

'Probably September.'

'Well, give me some time. I have some agents.' Munna left the room.

'How grand was the function?' Munni asked.

'The procession was colourful. I watched it from the window. A band was playing. Your dad arrived in a hired car. Several politicians attended, including one Minister. Yet my father was sad,' Amina Bi recollected.

'Why?'

'He was worried that his future son-in-law was unemployed. But my mother pestered him to accept your dad. They were cousins.'

'Meaning?'

'She was the daughter of your grandfather's sister.'

'What did you think?' Baby asked Amina Bi.

'Your dad was handsome, jovial and loving. I was only twelve years old'

'And he?'

'He was thirteen years elder to me.'

'Why was grandma insisting on dad marrying you?'

'The reason was funny. My father was a moneylender. He would drag defaulters to court. Naturally, they turned against him. Mother thought that as a local leader, your dad could protect him.'

'Was my dad a bully or muscleman?'

'I don't know. I was a child,' Amina Bi replied.

'Alright, did he really protect our grandfather?'

'Rather my father wished to have protection from your dad!' Amina Bi said half jokingly.

'I say, you are misguiding the children,' protested Jaffer Sharief.

'I know for certain that you were my father's debtor at the time of his death.'

'Does that mean that I was a threat to him?'

'Unfortunately, my father died early. On his deathbed, he held your hand and pleaded with you to take care of his family. Though you promised, you did not bother.'

'That was your duty. All my earnings were with you. Why didn't you help your people?'

'Unless you asked me to do so, I would not use your money for any purpose other than for your own children.'

'Oh, you are so saintly!'

'Do you doubt it?'

At that stage, Munni intervened: 'Please stop fighting.'

'Dad, is Munna born of Mummy or grandma?' Seven-year-old Babu asked innocently.

'What do you mean?' shrilled a shocked Amina Bi.

'They say that grandma was breastfeeding Munna.'

'I see. That was true. My youngest brother was still an infant when I gave birth to Munna. My mother used to feed both the babies. Till her death, she showed extra affection for Munna than towards any of you.'

Munna returned.

'I have traced the date of wedding,' he announced. 6 September 1957!'

What a surprise! It's ultimate value is nine, Shine remarked.

And Jaffer Sharief's favourite number is nine, Shade added.

For the couple it was an eventful journey from zero to nine.

FEMALE FRATERNITY

'JAFFER, HAVE YOU EVER noticed that hell hath no fury like a female betrayed,' Jasraj Kapoor began with no preface.

'But what made you remember this now?'

'You being younger have yet to learn.'

'I have some sort of an inkling that man does enjoy being doubted by his spouse, though he might pretend to be disturbed. To him, it is a proof of manliness,' said Jaffer Sharief.

'Smile and smile and be a villain. Libido has direct bearing to distance and strangeness. Curiosity ignites sex; familiarity blunts it,' Kapoor added.

'In married life, how could one sustain curiosity?'

'Try to relate sex with intelligence, wit, art, craft or any other such skill manifest in the partner.'

'If none exists?'

'Then God alone could help!'

'Are all females identical in their responses and reactions?' Jaffer Sharief enquired.

'Possibly. However, a sense of insecurity acts as a deterrent among the weaker sex.'

Their car had stopped at a traffic signal. Kapoor looked out of the window and asked, 'Jaffer, what is your opinion about the dress of the younger of the two dames crossing the road?'

'She has narrow shoulders, a small bust and broad hips and so her legs look long and lean in jeans.'

'You possess a cute dress sense. Have you done fashion designing?'

'I have an idea of tailoring.'

'I see. Clothes should flatter the body shape. One should choose clothes that accentuate the good parts and disguise the awkward. The other female has a big bottom and does not appeal to me for that reason. Her waistline is not well defined,' Kapoor commented.

'Yeah, she should avoid skinny pants and the pants should not go beyond her belly button.'

'I have a fetish about fantasizing about the outlines of lingerie of any walking beauty in the street. Do you have any?' Kapoor asked.

'You cannot call it a fetish. Mine is a savage inner urge. Whenever I see a shapely model with long legs in a swimsuit on screen, I dream of cutting out a piece of flesh like a slice of cake from the inner side of her thigh, chewing it and drinking the juice,' Jaffer Sharief admitted.

'You are a cannibal!'

'Call me anything you like; afterall it is a harmless desire. Fashion dictates that women spend more and more for wearing less and less. Less the lingerie, more the lingering glances.'

'Clothes helps them to conceal their real age. I gifted a sari to my wife on our last wedding anniversary. That left her speechless,' Kapoor said.

'Oh, so grand?'

'She stopped talking to me. Then she broke the silence to express a desire.'

'What was that?'

'She wanted to dance over the earth under which I was buried!' Kapoor said.

'Will you oblige?'

'I added my last wish in my will that I be buried under the sea!

'You are clever. It can go round as a joke.'

'If your partner loves, your life is happier; if not, you become a philosopher—this old saying still holds water. Jaffer, if not a philosopher, I have at least become a discoverer: inside the dress, every female is nude.'

They reached the Party office. Back in Kapoor's house, Mrs Kapoor and Mrs Jaffer Sharief were engaged in a dialogue on a diagonally opposite topic.

'What would you like us to talk about? Rain, rivers, mountains, deserts, flowers, birds, clouds, stars, moon, sun...Tell me Amina?'

Mrs Kapoor, effervescent and a feminist, encouraged her. Though Jaffer Sharief was very closely associated with Jasraj Kapoor, he had not introduced his wife to Mrs Kapoor. Amina Bi and Jaffer Sharief had been invited to the Kapoor's house for lunch. After a warm reception and sumptuous treat, the two men had left for the Party office. Mrs Kapoor was an interesting conversationalist. Amina Bi was a keen listener. They had a whale of time exchanging views.

'You did not choose a topic. Well, then, let us talk about a handy subject that is as simple as water. Could you guess?'

Amina Bi lowered her jaw.

'Oh, poor little girl, I meant the eternal enigma—Man. By the way, what is your opinion about men?'

'I have a man, he loves me and we are happy.'

'Have you studied him well?'

'There was no need. He does not pose any problem to me.'

'It shows either you are naïve or he is clever. Amina, take it from me, never trust a man.'

Amina giggled. Those days she was fond of laughing.

'I know you are sceptical about my observation. Man cannot but cheat his life partner. It is a congenital urge.'

'But Bhabi, this is a blanket allegation.'

'Right, there may be exceptions. There, the reasons are biological.'

'I don't understand.'

'I shall try to explain. Scientists say certain hormones released in man provoke him to cheat. This hormone makes wives less loved and less secure. We call it 'cheating gene'. That directs the production of the villain hormone.'

Amina Bi could not control her laughter.

'Now, come to exceptions. Those men who produce less of this mischievous hormone are gentlemen. But, for that very reason, they are looked down as subnormal.'

Again, Amina Bi burst into laughter. In between, she posed a doubt to the learned guru, Mrs Kapoor: 'If the hormone is the culprit, why should we blame men?'

'Quite right. But keep this information close to your heart. Don't pass it on to your man. These politicians will not read anything other than the news related to Gandhi and Nehru. Keep him on tenterhooks so that each time he thinks of the opposite sex, his conscience should tremble.'

'One more advice. Never catch your man red-handed. Even if you see him fooling around with a female, retreat tactfully and corner him only with circumstantial evidence. You should allow him scope for excuse and alibi. When he fumbles, you enjoy his discomfiture.'

'What will happen if we catch him?' Amina Bi was thoughtful this time.

'That will shock him. He will react wildly and unwisely. Some will explode; some will plead for mercy; some will declare independence; some will grant freedom. On regaining his balance, he might be immune to any threat or exposure. By catching him red-handed, you will be left with no weapons in your reserve. Don't commit that blunder. Man should be made to bend, but not break. Resistance and resilience vary from man to man.'

'Bhabi, right now there is peace in the house, but…' Amina Bi started applying her mind in the direction of safeguards.

'I don't doubt your sincerity. But your contentment could be an illusion as well. When a housewife says there is peace in her house, it only means that she has reconciled or resigned to her subordinate status in the family. Peace cannot be brought about without understanding, understanding cannot come without dialogue and dialogue cannot take place except among equals.'

'You are right Bhabi, but we cannot be equal to men. Nature has made us weak, dependent and insecure.'

'Amina, we should overcome this diffident attitude. Never allow men to take us lightly. Man has greater stamina but woman is emotionally stronger. I read an interesting example of male chauvinism. In the 1936 Olympic Games, Stella Walsh of Poland, known as the fastest woman in the world till then, was beaten by Hellen Stephens of St. Louis. Hellen set a world record by running 100 metres in 11.4 seconds. After the race, some Polish journalists protested that Hellen must be a man. They argued that no woman in the world could run that fast. Olympic officials performed the sex test on Hellen and she was found to be perfectly female. It proved that a person could be incredibly fast and female at the same time. Amina, our aim should be not to equal but to excel men.'

'In our families, the woman speaks out her wishes and man acts as he wills. Some doctors hang a notice on the wall of their consulting room: 'I treat, He cures'. But, there is a ray of hope. Come children, you could bank upon them provided you mould them to suit the ground realities.' Mrs Kapoor was at her garrulous best.

The bell rang. Jasraj Kapoor and Jaffer Sharief were at the doorstep.

Years later, Jaffer Sharief resented the fact that he had introduced Amina Bi to Mrs Kapoor.

SHE IS NO MORE

FORTY YEARS HAD PASSED since that visit to the Kapoors.

Ramu opened his eyes in the middle of a disturbing dream. It was well past midnight. Lying in bed, listening to the prayer call from a nearby mosque, he recollected the sequence of the dream.

After a journey, Jaffer Sharief stood in the portico of his new house. Many visitors were waiting there for him. Ramu, who had accompanied him, started walking back to the main gate. Hearing a commotion, he looked back and saw Jaffer Sharief lose his balance and fall down. As Ramu ran to him, he noticed a security man lifting Jaffer Sharief by putting his arms around his waist and carrying him through the hall to the bedroom. No family member could be seen. Ramu, who followed the security man, was shocked to witness a strange scene. Jaffer Sharief slipped from the grip of the security-man and fell down on his back. In that position, he appeared to have lost one half of his body vertically.

Ramu did not remember Jaffer Sharief appearing in his dream before. That evening he received a telephone message that Amina Bi had passed away that morning at half past ten!

She was sixty-three. It was just a week after her cataract operation. On that occasion, Ramu had visited her. Then, she casually expressed a wish that he should write her biography. She claimed that she was worth a book. After the eye surgery, while at home, she contracted lung infection and pneumonia. Though she had been a fighter all her life, she had finally succumbed. Respiratory tubes attached to her nose and mouth prevented her from speaking, two days prior to the end, though she was conscious throughout.

After 29 January 1999, death had revisited the house of Jaffer Sharief on 10 December 2008. That Wednesday was two days before the first anniversary of occupying her new house and six days before the first wedding anniversary of her grandson.

Besides Ramu, two other persons had premonitions through dreams about the impending tragedy. Wife of a former assistant of Jaffer Sharief was one and the other was a maid engaged in the bungalow of Jaffer Sharief when he was a Minister.

Amina Bi was in the ICU for four days. Doctors knew that she was sinking but did not convey that to Jaffer Sharief. In between she showed some improvement on the day before her death. As she breathed her last, her elder daughter who was beside her, came out and broke the news to her father, controlling her emotions and tears. Some well-wishers who heard it broke down. Before the situation went out of control, Jaffer Sharief was driven away to the house.

The plan was to bury her the next day. But it was changed and arrangements were made for the same night. People started flowing into the house where the body was kept for the family members' view. The funeral procession was massive and mournful. Among those who attended it were detractors, rivals, rebels and sceptics of Jaffer Sharief.

Amina Bi was laid to rest on the right side of her son, Babu. There was a thick growth of green grass over his grave. The six-feet long raised earth looked like a saint lying down facing eastward in meditation.

'Mother, you came so soon; Almighty is merciful;' perhaps these were the inaudible words one could experience from the air.

A heap of new soil covered the mortal remains of Amina Bi. A sheet of flowers enveloped her grave. While praying there, visuals of Amina Bi passed one by one along the memory lane of Jaffer Sharief's mind—a shy bride of twelve years old; a proud mother of four; a liberal provider to the needy; an erudite interpreter of religious texts; a sad spectator of the waywardness of the wards and a spirited fighter for life who finally beat her retreat majestically.

After prayers, Jaffer Sharief and team returned to the house that stood, for the first time, without Amina Bi. Surrounded by mourners, Jaffer Sharief could absorb the deafening implosion of his emotional blackout. Yet, he went on silently asking:

'Why did you jump the queue?'

BATTLE OF WITS

AMINA WAS NOT A silent withdrawn unresponsive participant in family quarrels. She was volcanic, violent and inflammable. Against Jaffer Sharief, she evolved a policy of carpet-bombing since the very beginning. In that process, the house often turned into a virtual inferno for him. Perhaps she did so because of his indiscreet moves or he did so because of her paranoia. Of late, she had developed a second habit of spouse harassment. However, the more she flared up, the less he reacted.

The young generation had never heard Jaffer Sharief calling his wife by her name. Instead, he used the respectful monosyllable 'ji' to draw her attention. Amina Bi, in turn, at the slightest provocation, called him, 'Oh, Jaffer Sharief' to underscore her superiority over him.

Jaffer Sharief was a toy for Amina Bi. She played with, talked to, threw away, cried off, tied down, locked up and sometimes let loose that toy. She did not want anyone else to play with her toy. If anybody came closer, she became hysteric.

She objected to him dyeing his grey hair so as to render him less attractive to the opposite sex. She forced him to grow a beard to give the appearance that he had renounced all worldly pleasures. In fact, she wanted him to grow older soon. She chided him for looking at the photographs of girls whose parents had responded to the matrimonial ad of her grandson. He was not comfortable to look at or talk to maids in the house in the presence of Amina Bi.

He took care to show fake detachment although she read his mind.

The house without Amina Bi wore a forlorn look. In the centre of the hall there used to be a swinging cot, carved in expensive rosewood, but now that had been moved to a side room. A large mirror with a fancy frame was fixed on one wall of the hall. A big television was fixed parallel to the mirror. Both the mirror and the television screen were now covered by white pieces of cloth. These two fixtures were virtually in mourning. Amina Bi, sitting on a sofa used to watch her reflection in the mirror and the reflection of the world on the television screen.

All the surviving sisters of Jaffer Sharief now moved freely inside the palatial house. In the presence of Amina Bi, they did not feel free to enter, without being invited. Now, they occupied any seat, stepped into any room and ordered the staff around. They had their blood pressure checked up by their brother's personal doctor. Had Amina Bi been around, she would perhaps have asked whether the house was a hospital. Above all, the sisters could freely converse with Jaffer Sharief now.

Jaffer Sharief's only brother was unable to conceal the excitement of his sudden freedom. Till the other day, his movement had been limited to the verandah, outside the front door. He waited there for Jaffer Sharief like an outcaste. He now moved inside with great abandon ordering and controlling the staff. He kicked away the slippers and shoes from the main doorstep, left by the unsuspecting visitors.

Conversely, Amina Bi's relatives, who had been privileged guests till the other day, withdrew themselves into their shells, all of a sudden. They felt the departure of Amina Bi as a bolt from the blue. They were stunned. They became strangers to the house overnight. Most of them kept away from the house. Two brothers of Amina Bi remained for a couple of days and then left. Perhaps they feared revengeful indifference from the other side.

The daughters kept their father company. Amina Bi used to complain that her daughters were indifferent to her. The daughters, in turn, nursed a grudge that their parents favoured their male children and their offshoots. Personal laws of religion are heavily tilted in favour of male children. They hoped to correct this imbalance by appeasing their father.

During Amina Bi's time, no one dared to complain or protest. She knowingly or unknowingly wore an aura of autocracy. Disagreement or arguments were akin to blasphemy in her circle of association. Jaffer Sharief could, at times, be taken for a ride, but never Amina Bi. She was a law unto herself.

As the eldest of Fakruddin Zehra Bi's eight children, Amina Bi was good at tackling the poverty of her early days and negotiating the affluence of the later years. Since she could read Urdu only, she spent her leisure time reading religious texts. Jaffer Sharief bought books from all available sources for her. Gradually, she acquired scholarly knowledge of religious matters. Maulana Ali Mia, the unquestionable scholar in Islamic subjects during his time, advised Jaffer Sharief, after a brief discussion with Amina Bi, that he should respect his wife.

ADIEU TO AMINA BI

THE POST-DEATH RITUALS WERE to last for forty days. Each day, a group of students from a religious school, led by their teacher from the seminary, came to the house, recited verses from the Holy Quran and left. During the first few days the house witnessed a flow of visitors arriving to pay condolences. The family members wearing simple dress, looked sorrowful and sober; they moved slowly and spoke in few words. Women camping in the house, to give company to the family members, gathered in various corners and chanted prayers. Jaffer Sharief, however, displayed courage and conversed with those who called on him. Some visitors wiped their tears, others cried and few people recalled their memories.

Visitors entered from the main door, removed their footwear and left them in the portico. At times, the entire area was littered with leather items. A few people entered with their shoes on, perhaps to save them from being lost. Chairs that had been kept in the portico would be occupied by early visitors and newcomers had to stand. They spoke in hushed tones. Even smiles were sorrowful. Loud voices were forbidden, lest they should offend the sadness of the surroundings.

Male members headed by Jaffer Sharief visited Amina Bi's burial place daily for the first seven days to pray there. Relatives and locals also joined them.

Days passed. Guest mourners started voicing their disapproval of the food served.

'The Quran does not forbid meat during mourning.'

The turbaned religious scholar gave the verdict while running his fingers through his long, dyed beard. The next day, the dinner plates that had been thrown into the washbasin had no leftovers, except bones. As the early formalities had been forgotten, the womenfolk lazed on the lawns, basked under the January sun, roughly calculating the quantum of property left behind by Amina Bi.

Elaborate evening prayers marked the tenth, twentieth and thirtieth days, and also the most important fortieth day. During those days the house looked crowded. After the prayers and dinner, the male members proceeded to the grave for prayers. Some also-ran mourners chose strategic positions in the circle around the grave so as to not miss the attention of Jaffer Sharief, which would be encashed later.

It was decided that the fortieth day function would be held in grand style, and as it approached, the activities gained momentum. Printing invitation cards, preparing the list of invitees, organizing the pandal, chairs, sound system and food—both vegetarian and non-vegetarian—as well as transport and accommodation of guests were all taken up in a tearing hurry. Whoever came, left with a bunch of invitation cards for distribution among the well-wishers. Using this opportunity, some of Jaffer Sharief's relatives managed to get employment for their wards in his office.

Jaffer Sharief suddenly remembered that the doctors who attended Amina Bi during her last moments should be invited. He started dictating to his steno:

'Dear Dr Devi Shetty, I thank you for the personalized attention that my wife received from you and your team during her last days. You have successfully saved her from a couple of such crises in the past. Unfortunately for this time, destiny decided the other way. We mortals are helpless. The last rites in her name will be held on the fortieth day of her death. As the person who watched my wife breathing her last, your presence here will fill her soul with peace. My wife had abundant faith in your care for her in the hospital. I am sure that ...'

Jaffer Sharief became silent. The steno looked up. He saw his boss struggling for words as he wiped his eyes. Asking the steno to complete the letter, he retired to his bedroom.

While coming out of the house through the central hall, the steno noticed that some women who would be staying there for a couple more days, had pulled a wooden stool on which they had drawn a country-style chessboard with chalk. They were starting a game with pebble pawns, watched by the other women with anxiety and anticipation.

LAST RITES

THE RITUALS ENDED WITH prayers at the burial ground. A small group of relatives and well-wishers joined Jaffer Sharief. Removing their footwear and covering heads with kerchiefs all reached the burial spot of Amina Bi which was adjacent to the grave of her son.

Jaffer Sharief had not given much thought to the need for space in the burial ground till the death of his son. But that tragedy made him reserve a piece of earth in the compound. The next occupant happened to be Amina Bi. Death does not observe order or discipline.

On the day before, a granite slab was installed on the head side of Amina Bi. Scriptures from the Holy Quran were carved in gold on the black slab. Eight years after his death, the colours had faded on the slab marking Babu's grave.

The burial ground was filled to its capacity with graves—shoulder-to-shoulder and head to feet. All graves were of identical length except for those of children. Boundaries were demarcated by layers of mud bricks. Several of the graves had no stone slabs. Seeing the burial ground convinced one of one's ultimate requirement of a piece of land, measuring only three by six feet. A visit to this place made one humble.

The fleet of cars stopped by the roadside. People converged around the graves of mother and son. All had covered their heads, some with prayer caps and others with kerchiefs. They stood with their palms folded and heads bent. Jaffer Sharief stood at the feet of

Amina Bi. Munna stood at the head side. In between were Wahab and Rahman. Priests started saying prayers in Arabic. Hundreds of flowers covered the two graves. Munna laid flowers, sprinkled rose water and applied perfume over his mother's grave first and then over his brother's. Being too weak to stand, an armless chair was brought for him. He sat in it for the remaining part of the rituals. Jaffer Sharief, despite his old age, chose to stand. The prayers were addressed to God to open the doors of heavens for the departed soul. Finally, both graves were covered by a sheet made of flower garlands.

When returning from this land of silence, some distance away, there appeared a procession. That was for another funeral.

Death has no holiday, Shade remarked.
Death has no death either, Shine added.

MEA CULPA

YOU, SHARIEF, VIRTUALLY LYNCHED me in the court.

Jaffer, you must make it an occasion for introspection.

No doubt, I was unfair to Balan in his old days. As you know, by nature, I am possessive of men and matters. I demand nothing less than undivided dependence on me. Nonetheless, I was yearning for a chance to repay my moral debt. Balan was a noble soul, sought after by others just for company. That made me green with jealousy. It was for this that he opted for a long spell of self-exile abroad much against his will. I craved for an opportunity to nurse him. I would have had him treated in the most expensive hospital. He deprived me of my dream. It was a clash of egos. Finally he humbled me with his death. While attending the condolence meet, I was squirming with guilt. With shame, I waded through the contemptuous glances focusing on me—Jaffer stopped struggling for breath.

Listen Jaffer I am inclined to doubt you. As one of the few surviving old time associates, Balan knew your days of penury and the days of luxury; he knew your days of restraint and the days of licence. Were you not uncomfortable, maybe in your subconscious mind, with his intimate information about you?

Sharief, you are crossing the limits!

By ignoring Balan, Jaffer, you caused a permanent dent to your otherwise straight looking conscience. How will others trust you? For that matter, do you really believe in selfless relations?

Sharief, I deserve this criticism. I deliberately avoided a one-to-one talk with Balan. He was longing for it. On a few occasions when I visited him, I took care to have a third person with me, only to deny privacy.

You are a coward. Even inadvertently, you don't mention his name in your conversations.

You are right, Sharief.

Bygones are bygones. Repentance helps. Try to draw lessons from each lapse. Jaffer, look at the sagacity of the soul of Balan; he did not blame you!

Jaffer heaved a sigh of regret.

After a brief spell of silence:

Sharief, do you hear the loud laughter of that lazy chap Ramu?

I do.

He seems to be handling his life lightly. He believes that he is an intellectual. He does have analytical acumen, but he wastes it over unproductive ventures like literature, music and art, said Jaffer.

I remember Ramu laughing all night in the company of a couple of his friends. They were there to see us off to Mecca. Our flight was in the wee hours. Watching the nonstop laughter session from a distance, Amina Bi called him and commented with remorse, 'Ramu, I too, till a stage in my life, laughed like you.' With an overtone of melancholy, she added, 'I lost that faculty somewhere,' Sharief recalled.

Of late, she did withdraw into herself. As is wont with women, she reacted hysterically to stresses and strains. But it goes to her credit that she did not allow depression to overwhelm her. During dreams at midnight, she would sob, 'Who robbed me of my laughter; who stole my laughter?'—Jaffer remembered.

Train wheels rolling along the tracks used to answer angrily: Jaffer Sharief, Jaffer Sharief, Jaffer Sharief....!

Why angry? Shade asked.

Those wheels were virtually the productions of Jaffer Sharief. He, as Railway Minister, had modernized and expanded the rail wheel plant. Those wheels had the courage and propriety to show anger towards him, Shine answered.

Sharief, Sharief, get up at once, Jaffar shouted.

Why do you awaken me in the dead of night?

A mouse!

That's all?

I am terrified. It's crawling across my bosom.

But you were not afraid of mice in the past.

These days I am.

Keep the doors open, it will run away.

That will invite more rodents.

Then learn to live with it. After all it is a mouse. There are people who live carrying field rats in their hearts.

Will you wipe the smile off your lips?

I swear, I am not sarcastic.

Do you smell a rat here? Jaffer asked.

Yeah, I am getting a greedy dishonest scent.

Do you doubt me?

You are addressing your own conscience, and you don't expect a reply. Don't allow such thoughts to tax your brain.

How do you connect greed with me?

A childhood devoid of love, care and security or an adulthood subjected to discrimination, exploitation and contempt.

How do they manifest in me?

At times in the form of being disrespectful to truth. Would it annoy you if I speak freely?

Never, go ahead.

It is not safe to trust you. Honesty is not your priority. With you, a word given is a necessity of the past. You sideline, mince, chew out or swallow it. Even a ragpicker will not take a broken word. Truthfulness is the aura of manliness. Only the brave possess it.

You call me a coward?

As I have already diagnosed the causes, that is not your fault. Moreover, this is the age of cowards.

Listen, the mouse is scratching the bottom of my cot.

Let us deal with it squarely.

Sharif took a ruler from the writing table and kneeled down to peep under the cot. Suddenly the mouse jumped down to the floor and stood still staring at Sharief. But it was an awkward position in which to wield the stick. Sharief drove the mouse away from the cot's protection. It bolted to a corner and hid behind the curtain. A determined Sharief inched towards the intruder. Jaffer followed him cautiously. Sharief holding breath raised the ruler above his head. In one stroke he pulled the curtain to one side and there was the mouse. Sharief was about to strike when the lights went off.

Damn it. Jaffer take out the torch. It is on the side table.

Jaffer switched it on.

Keep the torchlight focused on its eyes and I will crush it now—ordered Sharief.

The flash of the torchlight completely blinded the mouse.

Jaffer watched Sharief tighten his grip on the ruler, his eyes narrowing in concentration.

Oh Jaffer, what the hell are you doing? You switched off the torch.

Jaffer kept mum.

I know you, you wanted to save the mouse.

Yes, Sharief, I did. I am sorry. Don't ask me why.

Never mind, after a while the mouse will doze off in some corner like an unkept promise dulled by the dust of time.

AHIMSA

MUNNA LOOKED WITH COMPASSION at the two goats tied to a post in the compound. One was chewing the leaves of a tree, unaware of what was in store for it in a short while to come. The other was lying on the ground without raising its head. It was the seventh day of the birth of Munna's son. Arrangements were being made for the celebrations. The main ritual was the cutting of the hair of the newborn for the first time. Relatives and friends had gathered. The family priest, dressed in white, arrived. Munna lay in the back seat of his car parked in the portico. His driver was chatting with his friends a little away.

Munna could hear people talk.

'Be careful. Cutting the hair of the child and slitting the throats of the goats should be simultaneous. You should hold the hind legs of the animal tight. There should be no confusion. Show me the knife; okay these are sharp enough.'

That was the voice of the priest.

He saw a young man coming out, untying the goats and dragging them to a corner. One was resisting while the other was obeying. Now Munna heard the prayers being recited inside the house. He knew what would happen in the next few moments. He heard Jaffer Sharief enquiring about him. He wanted to escape from the scene. He opened the car door, came out, occupied the driver's seat, started it, backed it a short distance, turned towards the gate and sped away at a tearing speed. His driver stood watching him helplessly.

Where is Munna? The priest came out. He realized that Munna had disappeared. 'There is no use waiting for him', he said and returned to the house.

By the time Munna returned, dinner was almost over and the guests had started dispersing. One of them, a lady, stopped by the side of Munna to say goodbye. Munna noticed that she was holding a present that was obviously meant for the baby.

'Why are you taking it back?'

'I didn't know that dolls were taboo. The priest objected saying these are idols,' she was apologetic.

'Oh, that was it. Look at me. I am also a doll, eager to be gift-wrapped.' Pointing his index finger skyward, he continued. 'Even at a throwaway price, that ultimate customer evades me. After all, he is also a Mohammadan. He rejects dolls, accepts only souls!'

Leaving the lady dumbfound, Munna stepped slightly unsteadily into the drawing room and looked at his child sleeping in the cradle. He ran his fingers over the baby's head. He felt the bristles and simultaneously smelt the excreta of the slaughtered animals.

'I say, where were you? We were searching for you—Jaffer Sharief,' asked Munna

'Chand, in fact, I too was searching for myself!'

Then came Bakr Id.

'Saheb, these days people prefer camels to goats for *qurbani* on Bakr Id,' said the family priest.

Jaffer Sharief just listened as the car moved on.

'If interested, I shall fetch one.' The priest has a business eye.

'What is the rate?'

'Ten to fifteen thousand.'

'So costly; goats are enough.'

'How many do you need?'

'As many as last year.'

At that stage, Munna intervened.

'What kind of sacrifice is there in simply buying animals from the market and slitting their throats? The principle behind that ritual, as I understand it, is that you should experience the agony of sacrificing one of your own wards to appease the creator. In order to embrace that level of pious grief, you should develop an intimate emotional bond with the sacrificial being. Without that, sacrifice becomes a rank slaughter and you, a butcher!'

Jaffer Sharief did not encourage the topic. He put an end to it, by muttering: 'These are all symbols.'

A couple of days later, his house manager informed him: 'Sir, Madam is against our usual practice of going for large numbers of goats.'

'Why?'

'She feels sympathy for the animals.'

'Well, do as she says.' He appreciated her stand and guessed the influence of their son.

Next week, one day before Bakr Id, Jaffer Sharief visited the site where his new house was being constructed. After watching the progress of the work, he got into his car. He saw the contractor approaching him, dragging a lamb. He informed him that it was for sacrifice and as the owner of the house, he should bless the animal by touching it. Jaffer Sharief hesitated for a moment. Then, with pain in his eyes, he looked at the lamb and slowly stroked its forehead murmuring a prayer. The animal stood innocently closer to him and started kissing his palm. The car moved away.

Contrary to his usual habit, Jaffer Sharief remained silent throughout, caressing his palm, till he reached home.

HOOFPRINTS AND PUGMARKS

MUNNA WAS RELAXING ON the lawns in a garden chair with his eyes closed. A stray dog that had managed to sneak into the compound hesitantly approached. It halted just before him. He threw a biscuit at it. It swallowed it up and looked at him expecting more.

'I am disgusted by your greed. Now you want another biscuit! I committed a mistake by entertaining you. Helping means dousing the fire for self-dependence.'

Taking a deep smoke he asked: 'Did you have your per capita sex today?'

The dog closed its eyes.

'Why, abstinence or denial? If it is the first, I have no comment. If it is denial, don't worry, our judiciary will intervene; it is pro-sex. File a suit for restitution of conjugal rights against any passing urchin bitch.'

The dog yawned as if the topic did not appeal to him.

'Okay, did you have your per capita milk?'

The dog did not move.

'Oh, you did not. Inflation, recession, stagnation?'

The dog wagged its tail as if in agreement.

'Some cat might have lapped it up. Beware of cats; they are wily, snobbish, aloof, formal and possessive. Cats refuse to be on call. They exhibit a strong independent streak. Have you noticed, a cat will not take its food unless it is invited?'

The dog lay on the ground, pulling a long face. Munna lowered his voice.

'I am neutral between canine and feline, but I shall share a state secret with you. My father, Jaffer Sharief, likes dogs more, for obvious reasons, understood?'

The dog blinked.

'No, you have not. Now listen. I overheard him talking on phone the other day that he preferred pups to kids as the former did not demand, complain or argue. He said he could pamper his pet, he could cajole his pet, he could coax his pet and he could spoil his pet without being embarrassed in society. He found comfort in the fact that his pet needed no school admission, no occupation and no share of his property. I guess that on the other side of the telephone it was either George Bush or Tony Blair. Let them go to hell; they are all tall dwarfs.'

'I drink away my days and drug away my nights. My life is a constant struggle between the spiritual and material, between the promise of eternal redemption and the lure of temporal pleasures. Straight from the prayer hall, I rush to the tavern. I am alone in the crowed. You are a simpleton, home trained, grew up with no TV or CD and forbidden to visit nightclubs. But, I do not pity you.

'As I grew uncomfortable with the nagging solitude, I bought a wall clock with an hourly alarm. It kept on reminding me of the rhythm of time with its sweet resonant metallic ring. We became friends. It helped me feel that I am in tune with time. But alas, these days, I start hearing, in its alarm, the violent ring of an approaching fire fighting van or the panicky siren of a speeding ambulance. I removed the batteries of the clock. Now, it hangs on the wall without emotions, like the face of an Alzheimer's patient.'

After a pause, he continued the monologue:

'Will you tell me a story, a dog-lore?

The dog howled in a long friendly tone.

'Well, that was mellifluous. It was in *Raag Darbar*. I enjoyed it. I want to reward you. Next time you come, bring your advocate. I want to bequeath my ancestral shares to you. I will write my will in your favour. But on one condition. You should institute four annual endowments in my name. Out of the interest accrued awards should be given for outstanding performance in four areas—howling, barking, licking and pillar wetting.

The Doberman, chained at the portico, growled at the street dog. Munna reassured his guest, 'Ignore him. He is an upper caste among your tribe. He is warning me that you are an untouchable scheduled caste. Look at his stupidity. Though I have chained him, he boasts that he is my master. He claims that he is my courage and he is my pride. He believes that he has trained me to take him for daily walks, serve him food and clean his shit. He is a bastard.'

The street dog looked up.

'Yeah, it is true. He does not know who his father is. He is a mixed breed; a mongrel. In a simple term, a bastard! Yet, he is proud of that status! In ancient Rome, each one loved to be called a bastard. They believed that all illegitimate ones were fathered by Caesar.'

The Dalit dog stood up in excitement, shaking its head both ways in quick succession.

'See, the Doberman stands with its butt of tail tucked between its legs out of shame.' Munna encouraged the dog, 'Can you organize a rally? Here justice is only for those who agitate. We should fight for bringing about an amendment to the Indian Constitution. A clause should be added just below its preamble. By the way, what is your name?'

The dog does not move.

'No name? Okay, I am christening you—you are Tommy.'

'So, the amended constitution should read thus: "The nation shall look after all the needs of Challakare Jaffer Sharief Abdul Kareem and his guest, Tommy". Are you happy now?'

The dog sniffed the earth.

Munna threw a whole packet of biscuits at the dog and shouted:

'You dogs earn your daily bread by the sole virtue of being dogs. Now, leave me alone. Don't enter my world without scratching.

Run away, son of a bitch!'

Squinting against the glaring sun, Tommy obeyed the command. By that time, Munna had already started hallucinating. He created above him a canopy of the full moon from the blazing noon. Inside that lunar circle, he focused on an image of a deer. Then he shaped a spotted tiger out of a floating wayward cloud and let it loose after the deer. He sat keenly watching the game of the deer running for its life and the tiger inching towards its prey. Now both were out of the limited circle of moon. They ran across the galaxy from Taurus to Virgo, from Libra to Capricorn, from Sagittarius to Pieces... The race ended in Gemini. One jump was enough for the predator to grab its pray. Munna was anxious to know what happened. But, to his utter surprise, the agitated tiger and the obliging deer compromised. They violated the script of Munna.

'Cut!'

Munna, the director of the forbidden romance of fornication, censored the erotic shot.

'Damn it, thooo...'

He cursed the pair and chewed them out. He lay back and gasped as if in a post-coital fatigue. Slowly he closed his eyes. Time passed. When Jaffer Sharief called him he opened his eyes, and it was night, with no sun or moon. He looked for the tiger and the deer. They too had vanished. However, all over the expanse of the sky, Munna spotted hoofprints and pugmarks!

PISCICULTURE

'WAHAB, WHAT ARE YOU busy with? Recollecting the past or anticipating the future?'

'No Rahman, I care only for the present.'

'But the present is almost an imaginary veneer, inseparable from the past and the future. Do you get a toehold on it?'

'With one foot in the past and the other in the future, I hold the present between my legs.'

'Is it comfortable to hold it that way?'

'It swerves like the octopus that I swallowed alive the other day which grappled and grabbed the walls of my stomach giving a cute sensation.'

'What happens then?'

'To the octopus?'

'No, to the present.'

'The present on being released from the torn past gets you to the future.'

'Simply?' Rahman became curious.

'No, sometimes thanking, other times cursing, often without looking at, and rarely wiping tears.'

'Do you brood over the present?'

'Never, the present is the yellow of the egg. It mixes well with the white of the past. I fry it. By the way, what is your experience?'

'I avoid facing the present.'

'Shy? Afraid?'

'Perhaps both.'

'You are afraid of rejection?'

'I don't know.'

'If I had a constitution like yours, I would have frozen the present,' Wahab said.

'As if you don't do so now!'

'With some effort.'

'Okay, Wahab, will you train me to tame the present.'

'During the rainy season, water gushes from the upper field to the lower one through the narrow passage in the bund. In the night, the villager, with a country sword in his raised hand sits, concentration personified, at the edge of the passage waiting for the jumping fish to strike. He executes it with lightning speed. Each fish he catches will boost up his ego. If he fails to synchronize the movements of the sword and the fish, he misses the present. It is an art, craft and profession. You got the message?'

'Well, yes. Can I use a torch?'

'What for?' Wahab wondered.

'I have read that a sudden charge of light blinds the fish.'

'I don't know, better ask the fish itself.'

'Don't brush me aside. I am genuinely interested in fish. But I am not a success in fishiculture.'

'Rahman if I remember rightly, the art of cultivating fish is called pisciculture.'

'Thank you for correcting me. If I feed them more, they die; if I feed them less, they die; as I drain out old water they die; when I fill in fresh water, they die. It is not my cup of tea.'

'Well, do a course in fishing in troubled waters,' suggested Wahab.

'Dada is coming, let us change the topic,' Rahman said.

'You have already changed the topic to mere fish. I only wish that some presentable, but sluggish or foolish fish bite your bait!'

As Jaffer Sharief entered the hall, he saw his grandsons in animated discussion about the dynamics of fish curry!

'Look here young men, as grandsons of Jaffer Sharief, I am sure your topic of discussion could never be a fish drinking in innocent water and breathing out innocuous air. I can well imagine what you are suffering from. So, get ready, we will set out tomorrow morning to net in a mermaid for Wahab!' Jaffer Sharief announced.

'Dada!' Wahab went through the motions of resisting.

'No more licence to you for freelancing,' Jaffer Sharief was firm.

He had celebrated the wedding of Wahab in December 2007. Rahman had witnessed the occasion like a fish out of water.

'Next will be your turn,' Jaffer Sharief turned to Rahman.

'No, never,' Rahman objected like a reflex action.

'But, why?'

'Not all men are fools, some are bachelors!'

'Who said so?' Jaffer Sharief asked laughing.

'Whoever it may be, I endorse it.'

'Any reason?'

'Dada, I admit that recreation is one's right and procreation is one's duty to one's lineage. Nevertheless, tomorrow, I don't want anyone to corner me with a complaint that I violated his or her right not to be born in this wretched world.'

'It is not marriage that you need first,' a baffled Jaffer Sharief said.

'Then what?' an anxious Rahman asked.

'Counselling!'

However, Rahman's philosophy disturbed the thoughts of Jaffer Sharief like a lonely fingerling in a quiet pond.

'I am eager to become a grandfather.'

'Leave it to me, Dada,' said Wahab.

'You prefer son or daughter?' asked Rahman.

'If a boy, I will teach him the art of chasing and catching butterflies,' Wahab winked at Rahman.

'If female?'

Wahab grew pensive. Perhaps, he didn't think of such a possibility.

'Tell me?' insisted Rahman.

'I will erect a nebulous safety cell of parental vigil around her,' Wahab's tone was firm.

'What for?'

'To protect her from any adulteration by the present,' said Wahab.

'A male chauvinist!' commented Jaffer Sharief.

MALE CHAUVINISM

JAFFER SHARIEF SLOWLY GLANCED through the memorandum. The theme was as old as human history—man harassing woman! The President and Secretary of the Women's Wing of the local Congress were sitting opposite to him. Reading it, he raised his eyes.

'Sir, each day we receive scores of petitions from wives of drinking men, beating men, extorting men, molesting men, doubting men, cheating men, deserting men .... for dowry deaths, wife burning, child marriage, girl infanticide, sati worship and what not!

'In this male dominant society, a woman cannot dream of equality or equal treatment. What should we do?'

'Police do not intervene effectively. They don't register complaints. Without a FIR it is not possible to move court. This representation pertains to your area.'

'Who is the DIG in charge here?'

'Mr Nizamuddin.'

'Get him on the line,' Jaffer Sharief told his clerk.

'Mr Nizamuddin is on leave.'

'Try his residence number.'

The clerk connected the DIG to Jaffer Sharief.

'Nizamuddin, how busy are you?

'Sir, I am always free for you.'

'I have not met you for some time. If you have no other engagement, I intend to visit you.'

'Sir, instead I shall call on you.'

'Never mind, I am coming and I can meet your wife too.'

'You are welcome.'

'How about right now?'

'Any time.'

'Well I will be there in thirty minutes.'

'That is fine.'

Jaffer Sharief turned to the visitors.

'Come ladies, I am taking you to the DIG. Present your case direct by to him.'

Nizamuddin received the VIP guest with his companions and led them into the drawing room. Jaffer Sharief introduced the social workers to him.

'Today is my wife's birthday. I took leave from office. She hates pomp and show.'

'Oh, where is she? I must greet her,' said Jaffer Sharief.

'Please wait.'

Nizamuddin climbed up the staircase and disappeared. Few minutes later, the visitors saw him coming down carrying his wife like a pearl necklace strung across his extended hands. At first, the visiting ladies thought that it was an exhibition of love. They controlled their mirth. But then they noticed Nizamuddin carefully placing his wife on the wheelchair near his chair and arranging her sari pleats. She looked gorgeous, aristocratic and confident.

'Laxmi, congratulations! I wish you many happy returns of the day!'

Jaffer Sharief went to her and shook her hand. 'I am sorry I did not bring a gift for you.'

'Oh, your presence is the best gift. Thank you for the sweet greetings,' Laxmi said.

The other visitors were taken aback. Laxmi Nizamuddin had no strength in her legs to carry her weight. Her body below the waist was paralyzed. She could only lie in bed or move on wheelchair.

'Laxmi, what are you busy with?' Jaffer Sharief asked.

'I am busy torturing Nizamuddin. I have made him a perfect nurse. Man harassing woman is common, here it is the reverse.'

'No,' Nizamuddin intervened. 'She is my guiding light. I am lucky to have her in my otherwise dreary, meaningless life.'

'What are you reading now, Laxmi?' Jaffer Sharief asked.

'I have not completed reading Nizamuddin,' Laxmi replied.

'She is correcting the mistakes of spelling, grammar and punctuation marks in my life,' Nizamuddin added.

'I still don't know why this brilliant youth wasted his life by opting for an invalid like me. When he proposed, I took it as a cruel joke first. I turned him down with all the force at my command. My family members were nonplussed. But Nizamuddin was determined, resolute and uncompromising. I doubted if it was pity that was governing him. Finally I yielded.'

Nizamuddin sat looking at her bewitching eyes, listening to her sweet voice and taking pride in her self-confidence.

Laxmi continued: 'Today, I realize that the Almighty is merciful. He, I mean God, has compensated me for my handicap with such a gift that few could expect in this universe.'

The guests partook of the birthday cake. They bade farewell to Laxmi and Nizamuddin. Neither the ladies nor Jaffer Sharief remembered the purpose for which they had visited the Deputy Inspector General of Police. They looked up. In the cloudless blue sky, towards the western horizon, a sickle-moon lay like a sickly anemic angel.

OFFSHOOTS

HOW DOES THE IMMEDIATE progeny identify with the Jaffer Sharief-Amina Bi union? asked Shine.

There are four of them in the rhythmic order of son-daughters-son: Munna, Munni, Baby and Babu. It is such a well-knit unit that even after marriage none ventured to move away from the orbit or ambit of the parental nucleus.

But, Shade, perhaps the spirit of the wards remains maimed in order to dissuade a possible longing for freedom. They are like caged parrots with wings clipped.

You may be right. Amina Bi donned the mantle of the master provider and distributed Privy Purses among the kith and kin, so as to secure automatic allegiance.

And, in course of time, the young pensioners, with periodic hike in dearness relief, forgot their capacity to earn their own livelihood. Even if let loose, they could only flutter their wings and ruffle their feathers. A nebulous web formed between their fingers that curbed their urge to sore high. The sky ceased to be a temptation to them.

Listen Shine, such situations are direct products of affluence. Yet, there is a silver lining. Unlike in many similar families, these children are cultured, well-mannered, loving, compassionate and God fearing.

Could we view them feature-wise?

Only the last child followed in the footprints of Jaffer Sharief and displayed a flair for social work. That was not an area of inspiration for others.

How about their attitude to wealth?

Like a heretic, Munna neither welcomed wealth nor disbursed it. Munni welcomes it but does not disburse. Baby poses to be lukewarm and neutral. Babu collected and distributed liberally.

What is their vocation?

No serious pursuit of anything. But as avocation, the first showed a weakness for dreams. The second seemingly has selected eating and dieting as her pastime. As for the third, who knows what! However, the last, as a diversion to his vocation of politics, indulged in entertainment.

Except for the first, all resemble their father. The first is the odd man out. He resembled the father of his father, who passed away decades before his birth.

Family structure?

Amina Bi and Jaffer Sharief married both their daughters on the same day in the late seventies. Similarly, both the sons tied knots on the same day in early eighties. While they selected their sons-in-law from Karnataka, they picked their daughters-in-law from Kashmir.

Between the sons-in-law, the first pursued education for nothing and the second chased ambition for everything. There is a saying that if your father is poor, that is your fate; and if your father-in-law is poor, that is your foolishness. Here both the sons-in-law proved that they were wise, down-to-earth...

The first son-in-law, for reasons unknown, wanted to do higher studies in anesthesia, but he says that his wife seems to believe that he needs a crash course under some snake charmer.

It took place a few years ago. For paucity of space in the garage of the joint family, the compound of the new house of the first son-in-law was used for parking a fifteen-seater luxury van of Jaffer Sharief. When the son-in-law organized a picnic at a spot in the outskirts of the city for a team of his male friends, he telephoned his father-in-law and asked if he could use the van.

'Doctor,' Jaffer Sharief used to call him doctor, 'why this formality. Treat it as your property. There is no need of asking me.'

But unfortunately an informant of the mother-in-law happened to see the team travelling in the van and dutifully passed on the news to her.

'Who does he think the van belongs to?'

That was the involuntary reaction of the lady of the house. These words were carried, verbatim, back to the son-in-law by the same agent with equal alacrity. An annoyed doctor announced to his wife, pointing at the van: 'The van must be removed at once from this house or I will move out of the house.'

Initially, his wife kept mum. But pressed for her reaction, she muttered, 'Let the vehicle be there.'

For the second son-in-law life was a business. In any dealing, including those of an emotional and personal nature, his sole criterion was usefulness. His obsession was pure white clothes. Yet, he wore a black attire for a joyful event in the house of his in-laws.

'Why so?' His wife asked before they left.

'Occasion demands it,' he replied.

Munna fathered one son and two daughters; Munni settled for a foster son; Baby gave birth to four sons and Babu left behind one son and one daughter.

How do they react to situations?

All children lined up behind their mother in her vigilance of Jaffer Sharief on issues of carnal discipline whenever she feared that he might violate them. But they turned the tables on Amina Bi in unison when Jaffer Sharief was lying on the operation table in London for a heart bypass surgery. They warned her of their collective ire should anything happen to their father in the theatre. They had concluded that constant nagging had weakened his heart.

How do you assess the overall personality of each of them?

The first had a philosophical bent of mind. Second is a rank materialist. The third employs diplomacy in day-to-day life. The fourth functioned as an executive with a professional touch.

The first did not care for his mind; the second for her body; the third for her freedom and the fourth for his life itself.

Here is a scene, let us watch it:

'Oh, don't walk in the rain, Abba Jan!' The children shouted at Jaffer Sharief from the portico of their new house.

'I prefer to walk in the rain.'

'Why?'

'So that passers-by won't know that I am weeping!'

A vintage Chaplin! remarked Shade.

You are right, said Shine.

All this while Ramu was dozing off in his favourite cane chair.

Hey, wake up man.

Ramu opened his eyes, rubbed his eyelids and yawned.

Listen, without your help we have made a cursory observation of your master's progeny. Could you please vet it?

No, I am not a party to your conclusions.

Okay, leave the biological offshoots, come to his career offshoots.

His career family was not a large one. He had baptized a chartered accountant and an advocate as Parliamentarians.

Do they orbit around him?

They did at one time. Then, the first secured freedom. Perhaps for that reason he could rise up to the level of the presiding officer of the Upper House. He is no more a satellite now.

How did he distance himself from Jaffer Sharief?

Jaffer Sharief had dreamt that by promoting a seemingly mediocre person he, as the solitary spokesman of Muslims in the state, would have no challenge. But in the process of elevating his novice, he ruined the chances of some aspirants who became his enemies. They ganged up and made Jaffer Sharief bite dust for the first time in the subsequent election.

Did his lieutenant do nothing to check the disaster?

No, either he was incapable of, or maybe by purpose.

By purpose?

Perhaps, he wished to eclipse Jaffer Sharief so that he could step into his shoes.

Homo sapiens, Homo sapiens!

Among Homo sapiens, a sense of gratitude is uncomfortable baggage. It ties him down to his benefactor, and fearful of the latter's scrutiny. To circumvent this discomfiture, the easiest way is to attribute a sort of jealousy on the patron and opt for separation. Once the rift is established, the debt is deemed to have been written off.

Don't overlook the flip side of this episode. Just because you received a favour from someone, you cannot mortgage yourself to him lock, stock and barrel. In that condition, you will have to take on his likes, dislikes, friendships, hatreds, wars and treaties. A possessive patron is a thorn in the flesh.

That is true. If you treat your helpful deeds as investments, you are bound to earn profit or incur loss.

Okay, come to the advocate.

He was a childhood pal.

He cared to display his solidarity to Jaffer Sharief and to that extent had to limit his ambitions. He watched the rise of his colleague in the Upper House. To draw the attention of the latter, he had had to cry on the floor of the House. Just to try his luck, he pretended a kind of aloofness from Jaffer Sharief, hoping to hoodwink the higher up, but could not fool their prying eyes. The bondage was tattooed on his forehead.

FAKIR

WADING THROUGH CROWDED TOWNS, sleepy villages, narrow bridges, vast paddy fields, long stretches of barren lands, mango groves, vineyards, cactus thickets, and dense forests, Jaffer Sharief arrived at the spot. Set against the backdrop of wooded hills, a rock cave appeared. The afternoon sun tried its best to sneak into that hermitage. Twitters of birds broke the overall silence.

He left his vehicle and assistants behind and started to climb along a zigzagging footpath strewn with pebbles. Against the slanting rays of a soft glowing sun, his shadow grew longer and longer towards the east. Finally he reached the cave.

The fakir was meditating. He was sitting erect, eyes half closed, with flowing grey hair, long beard and a loose outfit. The thumb and index finger of his right hand were rolling along a string of beads, to the rhythm of his lips. He radiated a serenity that enveloped the surroundings.

Jaffer Sharief silently sat before him on the rocky floor. Time ticked away. The seer took a long breath, opened his eyes, looked at his visitor and smiled mercifully.

'When did you arrive?'

'A few minutes ago.'

'Are you hungry?'

'No appetite.'

'Are you angry?'

'Perhaps at myself.'

'Are you lonely?'

'I am afraid, yes.'

'Go on.'

Jaffer Sharief looked down. The holy man waited. After a few moments of silence, the visitor opened out: 'I have no peace of mind.'

'Why?'

'Children do not listen, wife doubts, cadres cheat, leader chides, friend deserts, foe ignores, body revolts, mind agitates, Jaffer clashes with Sharief!'

'Listen, my son,' the saint began, 'you are one among the very few fortunate souls, chosen by God to serve God's creations. Continue your duty. Handicaps are tied to your legs in the form of unsympathetic surroundings. Never mind. The Almighty is testing your endurance. Keep up your spirit. Be willing to accept more and more challenges. Agonies make one pure. Wealth does not beget love, peace or wisdom. Don't deprive your wards of the rich experience of poverty; poverty of food, poverty of power and poverty of ego. As for your grievance, remember, sacrifice alone generates peace. Exercise control over comforts and affluence. You are not late. God bless you!'

'If I move fast, I miss the wayside views; if I go slow, co-runners relegate me to irrelevance; the alphabet and grammar of contemporary politics have undergone a sea of change. Should I or should I not? This is my dilemma. I slide on the slopes of my dreams. They have gathered a thick layer of blue and green algae. I cannot run through them.'

'Jaffer Sharief your business is not merely running. The end mission is important. You must identify your goal and run at a pace agreeable to your stamina and will. I will tell you a small story. A youth joined a sprint contest. Of the two of his rivals, one was lame and the other blind. At the blow of whistle he pranced and reached the mark outdistancing the other two. But, to his disappointment, there was no applause. The puzzled winner confided in an elderly man who gave him some advice. He took position for a rerun. This time he kept the other contestants closer to him, held their hands and moved to the finishing line. As three of them reached the mark together, a big applause greeted him. Don't miss the message of this story. How far or how fast you ran is not so important as how you ran!'

'In the crowded world,' Jaffer Sharief lamented, 'its damp smell of isolation is nauseating. My days bear the stamps of missed opportunities, repressed passions and forsaken loves. I find no one who understands me and no one who appreciates me. I wish I could find someone to love me.'

'Oh Jaffer Sharief, being single is not so bad. Each person is alone on the earth. Born alone, growing alone and finally gone too alone. As you travel in any speeding vehicle, you observe the trees, lamp posts and pedestrians all moving against your direction. But my child, have you ever looked up? The sky joins you. The clouds, the moon and the stars all move along with you. What else you want?'

'I always have to postpone what I want to do for what I have to do.'

'At least you have to do something. Remember, the world will survive with or without you. You have no reason to complain. Life is worth just a few droplets of meaningless tears. Immortality is a mirage. You are a mere mortal. Be grateful to God for each moment of your life—sweet, sour or bitter! May all your actions be in worship to Him!'

The fakir lowered his eyelids; his fingers began rolling the beads.

Jaffer Sharief stood up, bowed, took a few steps backwards, turned and walked down the hill as if in a trance. The tip of the setting sun slowly sank behind the western mountains.

NADI READING

IN THE YEAR 1988, on 23rd of February, Jaffer Sharief, again became a Union Minister. He took over the charge of the coal ministry. That government lasted only for one and half year.

One night, he was clearing pending files at his residence with his private secretary. When Balan entered the room, he stopped work and began to chat in lighter vein. Suddenly he asked: 'Balan, do you remember our visit to Thanjavur?'

Oh! Mysterious and incredible, Jaffer. One year and a half had passed.

Jaffer Sharief looked at his secretary and narrated that incident.

'I visited an astrologer at Thanjavur. Balan had accompanied me. We concealed our identity. They call it "nadi reading". What they want is one's name, date of birth and thumb impression. They claim to have possession of palm-leaf scriptures of the past, present and future of each individual in the world. The problem is to locate the leaf from their repository that matches the seeker's details. It depends on your luck. Many return disappointed. In my case, they located the relevant manuscript within two hours.'

'Once they retrieve the scripture, one reads it and another translates. It is in ancient Tamil. After interpreting, they wrote, down the contents in English in a notebook and passed it on to us.

'Today is 23rd February, the first anniversary of my induction into this government.'

Saying this, Jaffer Sharief opened his briefcase, took out a small notebook, turned to a particular page and drew the attention of his secretary to a particular sentence, highlighted and underlined:

A turning point in your life on the 156th day from now. (The day had been calculated as 23rd February 1988 in the margin.)

That was a prophecy made five months before it happened, that is, in September 1987.

His private secretary, a practicing Muslim, asked him: 'Sir, is it not improper for us to believe in astrology?'

'Then explain why?' asked Jaffer Sharief.

While leaving, Balan went up to the gate to see off the secretary. 'Balan, could you give me the address of that place?'

'Why not. But be careful, wannabe touts will buttonhole you. That area is a bizarre market. You will be swamped by palmists, numerologists, handwriting analysts, tarot card readers, parrot fortune tellers and the like.'

'By the by, what else was in the notebook about the boss?' the secretary inquired.

'It was good that you did not read further. The palm-leaf has denuded Jaffer Sharief. It has skinned him alive,' Balan said laughingly.

'So, you are satisfied with the hindsight too?'

'Yeah, but I must warn you. Never go beyond a point. You will be lost in the cobwebs of rebirths which might offend all rationale and logic.'

'For example?'

'One medical doctor developed a surreal intimacy with one of his female patients. She was in her terminal stage. The pain of being unable to save her haunted him. Finally, he tried his *nadi*. It said that in his past life, his daughter was murdered in front of his own eyes. In his present birth, the daughter had come to him pleading with him to save her.'

'It sounds romantic.'

'On the way back from Thanjavur, in some tribal region, a small procession blocked our car. It was neither joyous nor sad. Jaffer

Sharief grew curious. When he enquired, an elderly man stopped at the window of our vehicle and explained patiently:

'It is a wedding procession. But the bridegroom is no more. He died five years ago of pneumonia. The bride is also no more. She died of snakebite three months ago. We believe that an unmarried girl is forbidden to enter heaven. The only solution is to search for a deceased bachelor matching her horoscope and conduct a notional wedding. Tonight, our boy and their girl will tie knot. The remains of the bridegroom are in the urn covered by red cloth, carried by his father, close to his chest, in the middle of the procession. The bride, in another urn, will be placed beside his and she will wed him as is the custom. Before dispersal, there will be a feast.'

'Saying this, the old man extended his hand and Jaffer Sharief took out a currency note. As he took it we saw bewilderment in his eyes. It was a note of 500 rupees. We moved on but did not speak to each other. Then Jaffer asked me why I was silent. I replied that it was a heart-breaking scene.'

Balan reproduced their conversation verbatim.

'How delicately they handle life! They don't abandon their loved ones. They mock at the death. Balan, I casually bumped into the memory of a girl who died as a spinster,' Jaffer Sharief had said.

'How old?'

'Age-wise she matches,' Jaffer Sharief replied.

'To whom?' I asked him.

Jaffer Sharief parried that question with a wicked smile and continued: 'Balan, you are sixty-five and determined to die a bachelor.'

'God, Jaffer, you are cruel!' I screamed. The lit cigarette flew from my lips.

'But Balan, why are you indifferent to the dreamier side of life? You are not a misogynist. Even at this age, you are a lady-killer. You enjoy being with the opposite sex. I know for certain that you are intimate with many housewives in your circle. Since their spouses know your limit, they don't care. You enjoy discussing sex.

You read erotic books. What I advise is that you must yield to a workable relation, lest we unite you with an unknown female of our choice, posthumously.'

I then opened out: 'Jaffer, you are provoking me to reveal my past. Just to escape from the advances of a royal family dame, I had to remove four of my teeth from both rows from the front. I was thirty-five then. Seeing me with toothless gums, she took off her slipper while I showed her my cheek. "You are not worth a beating with a slipper even," she had rebuked me.

'To demonstrate her contempt for me, the next day she took the hand of a mahout of the palace elephant and dragged him to her bedroom and slammed the doors. She did all that before my eyes.'

After a few moments of silence, I added: 'To me, sex is like a king cobra. I yearn to watch, but don't dare to touch. Perhaps, I have broken someone's heart in my previous birth and incurred her curse.'

'Shall we turn back and rush again to Thanjavur?' Jaffer Sharief asked.

'Jaffer, I am beyond the ambit of the radar of nadi.'

'And, under its armpit am I,' Jaffer Sharief lamented.

The secretary moved away as if in a slow motion.

CHIKMAGALUR

'BALAN GET INTO THE car, I must visit a friend in Chikmagalur. He has been hospitalized there,' Jaffer Sharief said hurriedly.

'Will we stay there overnight?'

'We can return tonight itself.'

In the moving vehicle, Balan asked: 'How far is Chikamangalore?'

'It is not Chikamangalore, it's Chikmagalur, meaning the village of younger daughter.'

'Oh, such a lovely name! We Keralites feel more concern for our daughters.'

'That is the legacy of matriarchy. Is it still prevalent there?'

'Not in the old form which was associated with the then joint family system. Today, the old pattern of boys migrating to girls' houses has started staging a comeback. That ensures protection and freedom to women.'

'Balan you are right. The value of a girl child is yet to be fully recognized in my society.'

'That is easily noticeable. You celebrate the birthdays of your sons and grandsons with pomp and show, but do not bother even to remember the birthdays of your daughters and granddaughters. Okay, forget it. While sharing your property, the ratio between male and female is blatantly unfair.'

'Balan our personal law is such.'

'Jaffer you are a consummate hypocrite. You are the master of the wealth you have earned, so who prevents you from treating your sons and daughters alike? Equal right is natural justice. Don't you believe in it?'

Jaffer Sharief kept mum and Balan left the topic where it was. After a while, he asked: 'Who is your friend in hospital?'

'You know him, Rasheed.'

'I remember, what does he do?

'He and his wife run an educational institution.'

'Um...' Balan kept mum for a few moments and asked bluntly, 'There is a rumour that their main occupation is human trafficking under the cover of education.'

Jaffer Sharief jerked up in his seat, 'I too have heard that but I have no personal knowledge. People say that Rasheed procures girls from poor families from the interior and initiates them into the flesh trade. Outside, they are all the staff of the institution. The couple has known me for a long time. They used to treat me with my favourite food. You know my weakness. But, if what we have heard is right, that is sad.'

'Listen Jaffer,' Balan said, 'I have heard a story, but I don't know if it's true or false. When Rasheed was in his twenties, he had to stay in a distant village for some business, for a couple of weeks. The inhabitants were mostly illiterate. He developed an intimacy with a woman whom he had engaged to clean his house. When she became pregnant, he fled the village. He was a bachelor then. After a gap of twenty or so years, he visited the place again; this time to recruit girls for his institution. He called it campus selection where the sole criterion was his satisfaction in the bed. On that trip, only one girl qualified. He left after giving her same cash in advance and directing her to report for duty soon. She took one month to do so.'

'When Rasheed arrived, he saw the girl waiting in his chamber. He passed a glance at her companion, an elderly woman. They looked at each other intensely. He got up from his seat; she covered her mouth that had opened with awe with her palms. "Selvi?" he asked and she nodded.

'The girl watching their expressions was puzzled. During the test and selection, her mother was out of the village and the broker had acted her guardian all along.

'Silence filled the atmosphere. Rasheed and Selvi were speechless. He stole a glance at the girl. Her papers showed that she was twenty years old. Her slightly squint eyes focused on him. Shivers travelled through his spinal column.

"How do you know him?" The girl asked her mother who did not respond. Then she asked Rasheed how he knew her mother. When he didn't reply, she wanted to know what their relationship was.

'Neither of them answered. The girl was in jitters. Finally she asked, as if a soliloquy,

"Who am I to you both?"

'Rasheed and Selvi kept silent, looking at the earth.'

'She was crestfallen...The girl went back with her mother to her village by the next train. On the third day, Rasheed received a postcard from her: "I came to you not unaware of the services you expected of me, but at that time I was unaware that I had been fathered by you. Your child is growing in my womb. I came to you, prepared to terminate the foetus with your help. Now things have changed. I cannot single it out for murder. Unfortunately, I am not strong enough to murder you. I wish to save the child to commit it. At the same time, I am afraid that if the child happens to be male, it could one day rape me as well, for it is of your blood. Who knows what sin I committed against you in my previous life! I have now decided to..."

'The girl consumed poison.'

Balan concluded the narration. All through the story, Jaffer Sharief sat with his face turned the other way. Balan did not care for his posture. However, he had sensed the discomfiture of his friend. Finally, as if awakened from sleep, Jaffer Sharief looked at Balan, yawning and rubbing eyes.

'Balan, I am sorry, I fell asleep. What were you talking about?'

'About the vast meadows, lush green fields, gurgling streams, flocking flamingoes, the ashes of merry campfires left behind by courting couples, idle cowherds and worked up bulls chasing obliging cows ...'

'Then I did not miss much.'

'You have not, and will not. Slumber is armour against uncomfortable truths. Some people snore, you did not.' Balan was sarcastic.

'Let us have a cup of tea.'

Jaffer Sharief asked the driver to park the car in front of a restaurant. It was on the outskirts of the city. At the table, Jaffer Sharief took a unilateral decision to cut short the journey and take a U-turn then and there. Balan did not ask him the reason.

While traveling back, Jaffer Sharief talked mostly to himself: 'Man is helpless. He is a tool in the hands of circumstances. There is no use blaming anyone. Victim, culprit, witness... all mere illusions.'

'Perhaps Rasheed knows it better. He prospered as a royal pimp.' Balan, too talked to himself.

For sometime they sat still. Then, regaining his sense of mirth, Jaffer Sharief broke the silence: 'Balan, did you mention a girl who committed suicide by taking poison?'

'Yeah, you must be keen to know her star and zodiac symbol. Well, I volunteer to lend my spirit to play a surrogate spouse to her, unmindful of the taboos of the almanac, if at all any. Let Jaffer laugh, and Sharief sob.'

LAL BAGH

HERE IS A NOTE penned haphazardly with spelling mistakes. This was recovered from an old tin box abandoned on the terrace of an old house of Jaffer Sharief. Termites have eaten away a major portion.

Shade and Shine tried to decipher it.

He was engaged in a conversation with his mirror reflection. The arguments give an insight to the mental conflict he passed through the night that preceded the vertical split of the Congress for the first time.

'What is your advice; should I or should I not? They want to immobilize Indira Gandhi.'

'You possess evidence of a conspiracy. By passing it on, you will be betraying your mentors. You must desist from doing anything that will make your integrity questionable; let alone the shock it might cause others.'

'I don't underrate your warning. But view the issue as a commoner. Why don't you think radically? I am in the midst of an ideological tug of war. On my one side is personal gratitude and on the other, the wider interest of the organization. My individual credibility might suffer. I must sacrifice it at the altar of the interest of the Congress Party.'

'I say you are rationalizing your evil design. How have you concluded that the interest of the organization is not safe in the hands of the leaders on this side?'

'I doubt their rationale, unity, ability and above all their acceptability. If they succeed in their mission, the Congress will wither away.'

'Is that a calamity?'

'It may not be. But what is the alternative? We have no viable opposition to take over. The country will collapse in chaos and anarchy.'

'I do understand your dilemma. Yet, I prefer you to perish as Karna than flourish as Vibheeshana.'

'That is not an appropriate comparison. I do not fix my eye on power. I may be ruining myself for the sake of the Congress. If so happens, that is my destiny. Come on let us move.'

'Oh, you are dragging me. No use of resisting, you are mightier!'

Shine, what was the evidence he was talking about?

Shade, some say it was an audio cassette which he played for Indira Gandhi in the presence of Yashpal Kapoor, who was her political secretary. After listening to it, according to sources, she was in a pensive mood. Next morning, she called off the Congress session abruptly, preempting her detractors from dislodging her from power.

The remaining part of the retrieved scribbling was not clear enough to read. It was full of corrections and overwriting. However, the remaining part of the action was history. Jaffer Sharief's role was decisive and crucial in the birth of a political party under the all-persuasive leadership of Indira Gandhi, said Shade.

Where others apprehend risk, Jaffer Sharief spots opportunities. He possesses an uncanny impulse to read the Sensex of national sentiment. Blessed he certainly was on various occasions with right intuitions, Shine observed.

Jaffer Sharief, indeed, is a visionary, Shadow added.

Agreed. Nevertheless, he paved the way for the family rule of the Congress. Was that really his intention or had he ever imagined such a scenario? It cannot be, but it happened to be so, Shine opined.

Do we not hear a distant laughter from the days of yore?

It sounds like that of Nijalingappa!

Who was he? Shade asked.

He was leader of the group that opposed Indira Gandhi in 1969. And he was the chief patron of Jaffer Sharief, Shine replied.

All said and done, by defecting to the other camp, Jaffer was betraying the trust that Nijalingappa had placed on him.

But, Jaffer has an explanation. He claims that he had the clearance of Mrs. Nijalingappa for shifting his loyalty.

Had the lady declined, he would have approached others on the periphery –

Like?

—the gardener or the driver!

As a man of conscience one cannot blame him.

As Union Cabinet Minister, he wished to visit Nijalingappa, who was in his nineties then. While agreeing to the visit, Nijalingappa conveyed that the team should not exceed six as he had only six cups and six saucers in his house. Jaffer Sharief honoured that condition but that did not stop him from leading a caravan of vehicles with escort and pilot, baffling the villagers along the narrow lanes of Chitradurga and parking the fleet before the modest house of Nijalingappa.

'Jaffer, you are lucky to get a vitally important portfolio. You must be dear to the Prime Minister,' said Nijalingappa.

'No, it is not love; it is sheer compulsion. The Prime Minister, Rao, knows that the Muslim community is behind me. After all, he is a Brahmin and therefore, farsighted,' replied Jaffer Sharief.

'Well, keep it up.'

While bidding farewell, Nijalingappa looked into the eyes of his guest and observed: 'You have not changed; the same old Jaffer!'

Which Jaffer? asked Shade.

We don't have very many Jaffers. And, Nijalingappa was a student of Indian history. A couple of years later, predictably enough, Jaffer rebelled against his Prime Minister openly. In that context, a newspaper carried a cartoon with this caption: 'Mere Jaffer or Mir Jafar?'

Could it be that this modern Jaffer was pricking the Prime Minister for promoting a certain foreigner? Asked Shade.

History revisits, replied Shine.

FOREIGNER

BALAN WAS IN A confrontational mood.

'Jaffer, I shudder to think a foreigner heading the government of India. I cannot digest the skin-deep arguments of the thick-skinned Congress stooges that she is married to an Indian; she is our daughter-in-law; she has produced Indian children; she took Indian citizenship; she cooks Indian food ...all such bullshit. Their vision is blurred. They mistake slavery for loyalty, that too to a particular family. What is your opinion?'

'Balan, you are a fascist; I don't find anything wrong with her becoming the Indian Premier.'

'Listen, Jaffer, you people believe that objecting to a foreigner taking over as our Prime Minister is reserved for Hindu fundamentalists.'

'Balan, it is not bondage to the family as it appears to be. Congress cannot stand without an icon,' Jaffer Sharief explained.

'I have seen banana plants standing with props. But remember, the prop does not flower. Here, you insist that the support should flower and bear fruit. Why don't you understand?' Balan persisted.

'Why should I? I am with the people.'

'Jaffer, you should learn to swim against the current. Otherwise, one day, you will miss the bus. I can see you left by the roadside and relegated to irrelevance.'

'Balan, you are opinionated; learn to respect the public opinion. I have complete confidence in her leadership.'

'Public opinion is to be built up. Public is mute. Jaffer, you are to lend your voice to it.'

'Balan, are you really a well-wisher of mine?'

At that stage, Hanumanthappa entered. He was wearing a milky white kurta and pajama with a black waistcoat. True to a Congressman image, he threw his hat into the ring in support of Balan's 'foreigner'.

'I say, Balan, if she is a citizen of India, she is eligible for any constitutional position.'

'Mr Hanumanthappa I agree. But as an advocate by profession, you must know that she is not only a citizen of India, but a citizen of Italy also. Italian citizenship is a lifelong status which is not disposable or terminable.'

'Who cares for such technicalities!' Jaffer Sharief added.

'So long as our Constitution does not forbid it specifically, we will support her candidature,' said Hanumanthappa.

'You mean to say that unless and until the Indian Constitution says that she, by name, is not eligible for premiership, you will support her! You people have no feelings of national pride and self respect.'

'Balan, we must learn to be broadminded from the Italians. The national flag is so dear to one. The Italian national flag was designed by a French national,' Jaffer Sharief said.

'Who was that?' Balan asked.

'I don't know the context, but it was Napoleon Bonaparte.'

'Balan,' Hanumanthappa joined in, 'we believe in the principle of one world, "*Vasudhaiva Kutumbakam*". You are a narrow minded, anti-Congress Hindu terrorist.'

His remark provoked Balan.

'Mr Hanumanthappa, you are like the letter "f" in the language of Iceland. At the beginning of any word, "f" is truly "f"; place it between two vowels, their "f" becomes "v"; before letter "l" the same "f" becomes "b" and when followed by "nd", that funny letter "f" becomes "m".'

'Poor Hanumanthappa, you are a chameleon. The other day, at a Congress manifesto committee meeting, I saw you practising this colour changing magic. Jaffer had arranged for a Tamilian boy to note down the proceedings. For some purpose, you called for an assistant from the sidelines. That boy, out of respect, came forward. Seeing him approaching you, you frowned at him. "No, you are an outsider" that was your comment.'

Watching Hanumanthappa laugh, Balan continued: 'Though you claim to be fighting for the black, which represents the backward, you remain mesmerized by the aura of white. Of course, you proclaim your solidarity with the black, by darkening your head and heart—head by a coat of black dye and heart by a coat of black wool.'

'I remember reading about an Indian journalist's experience in London. While calling it a day, the driver of Margaret Thatcher took leave of her, saying, "Goodnight, Mrs Thatcher".

'I compare that driver's self-confidence with the bowing and genuflecting of you folk in front of your leader. Such gestures are amusing to an average westerner. Pride and human dignity are sadly foreign to you.'

Hanumanthappa gulped down his discomfiture and cast a ferocious look at Balan.

Searching for a matchbox to light a cigarette, Balan concluded: 'I don't blame her. I blame the inheritors of the Indian National Congress. The two of you belong to that historic relic.'

'Amen!' That was more the voice of Sharief than Jaffer.

Suddenly, the lights went off. In the pitch-dark room, the three groped for candles and matchbox. Those were the days of power cuts.

'Just you wait a little while
The nasty man in black will come
With his little chopper
He will chop you up.'

Reciting that children's play song, pointing his finger at the other two, in turn, after each line, Balan concluded: 'You are out.'

In the darkness they did not know who Balan pointed at.

So did Shine and Shade.

Shade, who is not foreigner in this world? Mother and child, husband and wife, teacher and disciple, guardian and ward...all turn strangers on one occasion or the other.

You are right Shine. Going deeper yet again, sex without love is foreign to the soul and womb without faith is foreign to the foetus.

Yes Shade, tomorrow the sky could treat the sun as a foreigner, water the fish, fire the heat and light its shadow. What do you think?

A perfect Jaffer vs Sharief!

MATRICULATE

'SIR, THIS FILE RELATES to a transfer case. In response to a complaint by a certain wing of a labour union, the Station Superintendent of Bombay Central is under your orders of transfer. As he is, at present, on sick leave, the orders could not be delivered yet. At the instance of the local Parliament Member, you had subsequently withdrawn that order. However, the Railways have already acted on your first order. They have posted a replacement. The new employee, securing his release from his incumbent post, is waiting to assume charge.'

The confused Secretary of the Railway Board placed the file before Jaffer Sharief. He took out the pen, removed the cap, wrote down the orders, without batting an eyelid and passed on the file to the bewildered secretary, a seasoned bureaucrat. The orders contained only two words:

'Maintain status quo.'

The secretary wondered as to how skillfully the Minister, who was a mere matriculate, wriggled out of a puzzling administrative knot!

'Sir, this is a funny case. A retired constable from the traffic police is offering himself to the vacant post of Member (Traffic) in the Railway Board. He is a simpleton and believes that the Railway Board is a body like the Coffee Board or Khadi Board. Still funnier is the fact that a Member of Parliament from Bihar has recommended his candidature.'

'Oh, is that all? I have dealt with several such people.'

Jaffer Sharief narrated one such incident.

'It was in the initial days of my taking over the Railways portfolio. The euphoria had not subsided among the local people. In fact, it continued for a spell; for that matter, in the subsequent spells as well.

'At the guest house in Bangalore, I saw a man in the crowd looking for a chance to meet me. But, he could not be accommodated since my schedule was very busy. I noticed him standing outside my chamber the next day too. Yet, I had to sideline him again. The third day, when I returned to the guest house at midnight after a function, I saw the same individual standing outside the main gate. I sent my secretary to call him. Railway officials and political friends were around me even during those late hours.

'I asked him what he wanted. He looked around, moved closer to me and whispered something in my ears. I could not grasp what he said.'

'I want a second class ticket to Coimbatore!'

'Do you think I am a booking clerk? I could not help asking him.'

'Annoyed though I was, I directed someone to give him a pass. But that gesture opened a floodgate. I had a tough time coping with the requests for passes.'

Jaffer Sharief, after a moment, added: 'By the way, we should reply to the traffic police constable, enlightening him of the status of the Railway Board and the standing of its Members.'

The officer opened yet another case.

'Sir, this is an amusing case. A few days ago, a young man, approached you at the gate crying. He was howling that he was the son of a railway man. You were about to get into the car. You took the paper from him and scribbled over it "examine and put up". Since it all happened in a hurry, you did not read the appeal. It seems as if he is not in his normal sense.'

The officer lowered his tone and disclosed, 'Sir, he seeks the intervention of Railways to ensure that his wife obliges him in the bed.'

'What?' Jaffer Sharief exclaimed.

'Yes, Sir. He claims that his father is exploiting his wife.'

Looking into the amused eyes of the officer, Jaffer Sharief said,

'Listen, you cannot brush it aside as a bedtime story. Nuances of human misery need careful handling. As that boy states, if his father is a railway employee, the elder's moral turpitude should be probed. I know a case where a domineering father forced the gullible son of his second wife to tie the knot with the old man's keep, thereby cheating his son. Unlike that father, I remember another father, who, days before his retirement, committed suicide in such a way that it would look like an accident. He made that supreme sacrifice to help his unemployed son get a job, on compassionate ground. I don't conclude that this is a similar case. But my advice to administration is always to keep by the side of the helpless and hapless. Bureaucracy needs the guidance of politics.'

As the bureaucrat walked down the long corridor back to his room, he felt nothing but awe and respect towards that politician who was only a matriculate.

Shine, we have been witnessing the phenomenon of rustic common sense leading manicured bureaucracy along the slippery slopes of human realities, observed Shade.

Oh, mother Democracy, praise to thee, said Shine.

Set against these Sharifian words of wisdom are the nonchalant transgressions of Jaffer—added Shine.

Can you recall one?

One of the maids at the residence had half a dozen children. She was obviously above forty and sluggish with a body weight of over a hundred kilograms. Mrs Jaffer Sharief recommended that she be given a job in the Railways. Jaffer readily agreed and directed the department to absorb the maid. But, the Railways returned the file recording the non-advisability of the proposal citing rules regarding age and drawing attention to the existing position of no vacancy and surplus staff. Jaffer took this as an act of disobedience. Enraged as he was, he overruled all the objections, reminded the administration of its primary commitment to the upliftment of the poor and the need of helping the weaker sex. He then ordered that if there was no other vacancy, his maid should be adjusted against sports quota! An amused Railways accepted her.

'I am the government,' beamed a triumphant Jaffer. 'Don't you appreciate my kind deed?' he asked Sharief.

'A deed of kindness for an outsider in the daylight shields hundred deeds of favouritism to insiders in the dark,' muttered a frustrated Sharief.

BLIND GOD

A VISITOR ENTERED JAFFER Sharief's chamber. He was assisted by a woman and a child. She led him to a chair, placed opposite the minister. The young man, who wore a pair of dark glasses, was blind.

'Sir, I am an ex-serviceman. These are my wife and daughter.'

'Be comfortable Baby, you are cute to look at. What is your name?'

'Jyothi, but children call me daughter of blind.'

Jaffer Sharief closed his eyes. After a few moments he asked:

'How did you lose your vision young man?'

'A land mine blast. I was returning to my base camp along the western boarder. It was midnight. Some mines had escaped the detection squad and one exploded just under the engine of the truck that I was driving. When I regained my consciousness, I realized that I would not see the world anymore.'

Offering him a glass of water, his wife said, 'Our child was only twenty-one days old on that day. He was dying to have a glimpse of her. His leave had already been sanctioned. He was to proceed to home the next evening. I was waiting to receive him with pride. And now...! He will never see his daughter. He cannot see her complexion, he cannot see the colour of her skirt. And he cannot see her smile.' She could not continue.

He sat there controlling his emotions.

Jaffer Sharief went through their appeal and recorded his order in the margin itself. Calling the officer concerned to his chamber, he directed, 'Accord priority to this matter and report compliance within fifteen days.'

Then he turned to the visitors, 'How did you come?'

'By bus.'

He called his private secretary and instructed him to provide a vehicle for their return.

The ex-soldier stood up. The minister shook his hand, waved at the lady and caressed the forehead of the girl.

Before leaving, the blind young man halted at the door, turned to the direction of the Minister and asked, 'Sir, you said my daughter is pretty. Did you mean it? How does my child look? I can only hear her.'

Jaffer Sharief was mum. His tongue dried up. He was at loss for words. The father was waiting for a reply. He struggled. 'Oh! Your daughter is as pretty as an angel. As a child of a jawan who sacrificed his eyesight for the sake of our motherland, she is more beautiful than any other. I am sure Jyothi will grow to be a *jyoti* for you.'

'Thank you, Sir.'

They moved out.

Jaffer Sharief instructed the door-keeper not to allow entry to anyone for some time. He sank into the chair which produced a screeching noise as if someone was wailing in pain. He put his head back; cupped his face with the hands; closed his eyes and whispered,

'Oh! God! Are you blind?'

A DIVINE VISITOR

MOTHER TERESA FLOATED INTO Jaffer Sharief's chamber like a lean, light film of milky white December cloud. Her usual blue-bordered white sari covered her forehead. The radiant face had a thousand wrinkles like tributaries and re-tributaries of glaciers of mercy. Her body was bent slightly forward. She was accompanied by a couple of the inmates of her hermitage. Jaffer Sharief felt illuminated by her divine presence. He fumbled as he did not know how to wish and receive her.

Mother held the hands of Jaffer Sharief. He became a child before her. He reverently looked at the wooden crucifix hanging around her neck.

In the corridor, there was a crowd eager to have a glimpse of the angel.

Jaffer Sharief carefully listened the words of the Mother. She passed some papers to him. She was seeking the goodwill of the Railways in facilitating the humanitarian service she was engaged in.

'My son, I have come to you with some desires to be fulfilled.' She smiled looking at his face and continued: 'When desires are unfulfilled the mind gets restless. When they are realized, greed sets in. Then you grow anxious to cater to the demands of greed. This is where arrogance seeps in and you start looking contemptuously at others poorer than you, and envy those who are better than you. Simultaneously, the fear of losing what you have engulfs you.'

The Mother stopped for a moment and began:

'This is how desires work at the level of individuals. But the same emotion of desire becomes desirable when it crops up to serve the interests of society. What I mean to say is that no feeling is taboo or negative if harnessed for the good of environment. That is my mission. If you could evince interest in such desires, I will thank Him.'

'Mother, how about jealousy, hatred and anger?' Jaffer Sharief asked.

'Be jealous of the pavement dweller who sleeps soundly lying half covered, in the midst of street animals; be hateful at the affluent who suffers sleepless nights in the coziest of beds despite an overdose of sedatives; be angry at the social system that widens the gulf between the haves and have-nots.'

Mother Teresa reminded Jaffer Sharief that he was the chosen Lamb of God to serve the humanity. It was his duty to look after the orphans, destitute, disabled, sick, aged and backward. He recalled the words of the fakir whom he visited some years ago. He too had observed so.

'My son,' the Mother said, 'if you can discern the right from the wrong, you are only at the halfway mark. To reach the destination, you must have sufficient will power to persist on the path of wisdom.'

Praying for strengthening the wisdom and will power of Jaffer Sharief, the Mother bade farewell. She walked as if the earth should not be hurt.

Jaffer Sharief felt as if he had been immersed in an evening raga flowing from a mellifluous shehnai of Varanasi. He returned to his seat with his spirit overflowing with peace and tranquility. Then he saw a card left on the table lying parallel to his bosom. He took it and read it. It was a prayer:

'Thou knowst everything Beloved. Let thy will always be done. In joy and sorrow, my Beloved, let thy will always be done.'

ROYAL FEAST

SO SHARIEF, YOU HAVE been keeping me locked up in a dark room? The tone of Jaffer betrayed annoyance.

Jaffer, you were longing for a sound sleep. I took care to see that none disturbed you.

Any new developments?

Mother Teresa graced Rail Bhavan office.

Then?

Maulana Ali Mia Saheb granted an interview. He was similar to the fakir in the far away cave. Ali Mia was sad about the miserable condition of Indian Muslims. He stressed the need to uplift them from their present poor social, educational and economic state. He has answers for all doubts that are spiritual and intellectual. He has a global following that wait for each of his words. By far, he is the tallest theologian on the Islamic faith today.

Well, now I have got up. Let me assume the power from you. I am coming out. Keep out of my way. This is the Ramzan season. To begin with, I am going to throw an iftar dinner such that the capital has not witnessed so far. There is enough balance in the hospitality fund of the Railways. The dinner will extend for three days.

But Jaffer, for whom? Sharief was clueless.

On the first day for the envoys of all foreign missions; second day for officials and media and the third day for Party men, friends and well-wishers.

As you like. But do you think any purpose will be served? Will such an un-Islamic bash generate any goodwill for the country, abroad?

I am confident, stated Jaffer.

Shortest route to heart is not through the stomach, grumbled Sharief.

He asked again: Will the heavens be pleased as the whole extravaganza is in the name of the Almighty?

I believe they will be, Jaffer said.

May your belief save you! One more question. Who do you hold the most respectable among the living learned today?

Maulana Ali Mia Saheb, said Jaffer.

Right. Suppose you had sought the opinion of Maulana Ali Mia Saheb, would he have approved of this show?

Jaffer remained mum for a few moments.

I don't know his tone was hesitant.

But I know and I know that you too, know. Sharief added in a sad tone. Knowledge is agony; the ignorant is lucky!

Witnessing the exchanges, Shade conferred with Shine:

Jaffer cannot afford the luxury of austerity.

In other words, it is the innocence of an imperial ego, Shine remarked.

Is it a psychic urge? asked Shade.

Urge for lavishness could be in the blood, said Shine.

The exercise evoked mixed reactions. However, regulars like drivers, clerks, cooks, peons and police did justice to the carnival by wolfing down the food, greedily. As a result, they had to face the mutiny of the intestines the fourth day. They had to employ purgatives to flush out the rebellious hospitality of the railways.

Years later, remembering it, Jaffer must have laughed, remarked Shine.

And Sharief wept, Shade added.

ON THAT FRIDAY…

'BROTHERS,' ADDRESSING THE OCEAN of wounded humanity before him, Jaffer Sharief began his speech at Lucknow in a tone filled with anguish, anger and sorrow. 'We Muslims, stand devalued today. Our hearts are bleeding. Our pride was demolished the other day. Today, we look towards sky and ask, "where is our Babri Masjid?" Our holy places have no protection in this land. The Babri Masjid was not just a masjid; it was not a mere building; it was not a historic monument; it was a symbol of Muslim existence in India. We identified it with our heritage and our contribution to the culture of this nation. Today, we feel that we are a minority in all respects in India. It is a painful status. How will we face our innocent children? The future will not forgive us for not protecting our past.'

'I hold that the government of the day failed in its duty of safeguarding the minority here. I suspect willful indifference. This act of commission is unacceptable. As a member of that government, I feel ashamed, I feel guilty and I feel betrayed.'

'To conclude, I warn those at the helm of affairs, never take the Muslim community for granted. I am with the community. If it so ordains, I will be with it to pull down this government of which unfortunately I too am a member.'

A thunderous applause greeted these words. 'Jaffer Sharief Zindabad' slogans filled the air. People surged forward to kiss his palm. The crowd grew hysteric. This speech was widely covered in the media.

Then came a Friday.

'Sir, a visitor from Ayodhya has been camping in Delhi for the last three days. He comes here every day. In one of your tours of Uttar Pradesh, he approached you seeking help for his heart operation. You, he says, referred him to a hospital in Lucknow and paid a hospital charge of over two lakh rupees. Now that he has regained his health, he wants to pay respect to you. His name is Laxman Singh,' his private secretary conveyed.

Jaffer Sharief was getting ready for Friday prayers, but he obliged.

Laxman Singh entered holding his folded hands skyward, above his head. He was gratitude personified. Overcome with emotions, he could not speak. His eyes were overflowing with tears. Instead of sitting in the chair the Minister offered, he moved to the side of the table and fell at the feet of Jaffer Sharief. An embarrassed Minister somehow persuaded him to take the seat. Then he enquired about the health of Laxman Singh and welfare of his wife and children.

Laxman Singh knew that the Minister was getting late for his Friday prayers.

'Sir, I have a desire to place before you. You are my living God. But for you, I would not have remained on earth. Before seeing you, I had knocked at very many resourceful doors, but everything was in vain. I still remember my first meeting with you. Observing my condition, I was unable to speak then, within moments you ordered my hospitalization. Had I been late for few more days...' Laxman Singh wept.

'Laxman Singh, I must leave now. I am getting late for the prayer time.'

'Sir, I am unable to express my thanks. I am poor; I have nothing to give you in return. I have decided to embrace Islam with my wife and children.'

'What did you say?' Jaffer Sharief was dumbfounded.

'Yes, Sir, you must bless me and my family. We want to become Muslims.'

Jaffer Sharief, sat down again, covered his face with both hands and remained in that posture for a couple of moments. Laxman Singh waited for his compliments. When Jaffer Sharief removed his hands, his face had turned red. He looked straight into the eyes of the visitor and roared: 'Get out!'

Laxman Singh was in jitters. He stood up.

'I say, get out of my sight. You thought that I would be thrilled to know your conversion plan. People like you are a disgrace to society. You are prostituting your own faith. I don't want to entertain or associate with anyone who has no respect for one's own culture and heritage. What a way you chose to please me! I repeat, kindly get out!'

Hearing the commotion inside, the personal security officer of the Minister peeped in. Jaffer Sharief called him and directed him to physically evict the visitor from the chamber at once.

Left alone, Jaffer Sharief prayed in silence: 'Oh, God, forgive me. I missed my Friday prayers.'

A MUCH MALIGNED SOUL

JAFFER, IT IS SICKENING to move about with our arms around each other's shoulders like Siamese twins.

I too feel the same monotony, Sharief. Let us lie down on the lawns and enjoy this evening sun.

I have been wondering why we are unable to preserve a long-standing friendship with anyone. Could it be an inbuilt deficiency?

As I look back, I get perplexed. Hundreds of acquaintances withered away leaving behind no souvenirs. Most of the relationships died down, ruing, lamenting, or loathing due to fading charisma on either side.

After each separation, we blame others of selfishness, greed, opportunism, treachery, betrayal and non-utility.

You and I are the culprits.

Why do you mention me first? Jaffer objected.

That is the command of the grammar, Sharief replied.

Long live grammar!

On many occasions, even sex does not sustain the curiosity.

It is a strange phenomenon. Nonetheless, this situation could suggest that seemingly intimate associations are often devoid of desire. You may pretend that your libido is irresistible, but behind the doors, you could be discussing the prices of vegetables.

Sharief, enough of this exposure. Kindly don't undermine the image that I built up with time. I don't wish to be portrayed as unlettered at least in this area. The truth, however, remains that I have not outraged the modesty of others.

So you are the proverbial frog in the pond?

A teetotaller frog!

Now, I realize, why you were pulling up some of your staff who were going wayward in the twilight of their youth.

There you are. They must be grinning and grumbling that their boss had little moral right to raise his eyebrows. But, the fact is otherwise. I do not cross the limit of morality. I am rightful to insist on a reasonable degree of conscientiousness among my subordinates.

I see; your nonchalance so far was puzzling to me. Now I realize that it originates from your inner righteousness.

You are right—Jaffer merged into Sharief. Sharief felt the warmth of a soft ache in the heart of Jaffer who was wandering through the misty corridors of his past.

Watching this scene, Shine confessed:

Shade, here is a much-maligned soul!

Do you remember; once, after a closed-door encounter with a damsel, who was reminiscent of a femme fatale of the emergency days, Jaffer came out holding a newspaper and asked the sleepy guard in an agitated tone:

'I say, what are the Americans up to?'

The shaken up cop blinked as he could not grasp the context. He was in jitters, fearing that the female inside could be a Yankee spy.

'Sir, anything serious?'

'Look at this report. The US moves to slap sanctions against Iran!'

'Yes, yes,' the relieved gunman nodded his head.

Our friend was in a global moral cop mode!—Shine observed.

But, then, what was he doing inside?—Asked Shade

Obviously, reading the *Hindustan Times*!

But, Shine, is Jaffer such a puritan?

He is, if one goes by what the informed sources say.

If so, they do a service to him. It is equal to a medical certificate.

Who are they? You mean the Bombay middleman in the movie circle?—Shade quizzed.

No!

That Calcutta broker in the political circle?

No!

That Madras agent in the business circle?

Let me hasten to reveal, lest you expose Jaffer. There was a guy from Jordan. He operated here in the guise of a medical student. He overstayed his visit with the connivance of politicians. He befriended them through brothels. He didn't hesitate even to enact live shows for them. He mastered the art of trapping females for satiating own lust and of his patrons.

Listen, Shine,—Shade continued—to encourage an alien to partake in sex is tantamount to outraging the modesty of our womanhood. This does not mean at all that natives could run amuck.

You are right, Shade. Trading with the pride of one's own motherland is nothing but sheer treason. One might fear that this issue is far fetched. But it is not so. On one of his visits to Jordan, Jaffer casually enquired about adult entertainment there. By that time, the latter had resettled in his homeland. Do you want to know how that cat-eyed Jordanian preempted Jaffer.

'Never ask for such service in Jordan. It is a sin here. We strictly follow the Shariat. Moreover, I have a name in this society. Wait, till I come to India. I will organize a variety of fun there.'

The story is not over. The Jordanian kept his word. He visited India. While returning after a pleasure trip, Jaffer and the Jordanian indulged in an erotic dialogue in a moving car:

'Why did you stay back?' asked the Jordanian who was behind the wheel.

'Oh, you know me; I don't go beyond a limit. How did you feel?' enquired Jaffer.

'She had a grip. Indian females generally lack that trick.'

'How does one gain that muscle management?' Jaffer was curious.

In the meantime, they tried to overtake a slow moving bus ahead of them. All of a sudden, some substance hit Jaffer's face. The windowpane of the car had been rolled down. A startled Jaffer looked at the Jordanian who saw blood on the eyes, cheeks and lips of Jaffer He shrieked in horror and stopped the car by the roadside. Jaffer wiped his face. Only then did they realize that it was not blood. What hit his face was a mouthful of thick spit ejected by a careless or mischievous passenger who was chewing betel leaves with tobacco.

Jaffer Saheb, don't get upset. We will chase and catch that guy. The bus is at a reachable distance from us—The Jordanian was about to speed up the car.

No, leave it. Let us go home—Jaffer discouraged his friend.

Shade, who could be the protester?

Shine, I have seen. The one who did it is well known to you, me and, mark my word, Jaffer too!

How come? Who was that?

That was none other than Jaffer's other self, Sharief! Who else would have the courage to attack Jaffer?—Shade revealed.

That is why Jaffer held back his companion from chasing the bus—Shade added.

As a protest, one could conceive no better a form—Shine.

Okay. Come to our original topic. What is the revelation of the Jordanian about Jaffer?

Shine, hold your breath—our hero derives pleasure in sharing experiences through conversations in bedroom privacy and offering help, if need be.

Did I not tell you? He is a gentleman.

DREAMS

JAFFER SHARIEF WAS SHIFTING from his Tughlak Road bungalow to Akbar Road. Heaps of waste papers had collected in the vacated house. Balan saw a notebook among them. Out of curiosity, he picked it up and flicked through the pages. Jaffer Sharief was not in the habit of writing diary. But his scribbles were in the notebook. His handwriting was clean and attractive. Under the date, 5 August 1982, he had written about one of his dreams:

Last night Meena Kumari appeared in my dreams. Before going to bed I had been watching a videotape of a movie in which she was the heroine. In the dream, she called me from a distance. While rushing to her, I lost my concentration and entered a wayside flat. A group of air hostesses stayed there. Balan was with me. The inmates, though gloomy, received us at the portico and led us into the drawing room. There lay a dead body in a coffin. I laid a wreath. Then I turned to a mourner and asked: where is she? 'She is in Taj; Room 343.' I ran to the Taj and knocked at the door. 'Who is that?' it was her voice. I got excited. Again I knocked without giving my name. Finally the door opened. I was taken aback and ashamed to see my driver in the bed.

'Ministry formation is going on. You are to be inducted. I am celebrating that event and you are knocking at this door,' he chided me.

Now, I am rushing to Rashtrapati Bhavan for my swearing-in. At the gate, I quarrelled with the security for securing entry to my companion. That was a girl working as a dish cleaner in the Parliament House canteen. She claimed to be daughter of a deceased MP. She was unwashed, unchanged and unkempt. She demanded a guard of honour from the security staff. Finally they yielded. In the melee outside, the swearing-in ceremony got over and I lost a berth in the Cabinet. When I returned to my flat in North Avenue, I saw a huge female drying her wet sari on a crowbar inside. She claimed to be a doctor from Gurgaon. I told her that that was my flat. She abused me in her metallic voice and pushed me out and closed the door. I called my clerk and dictated a complaint to the Chief Minister of Pondichery saying that that lady was being harassed by her sister's husband.

At this stage I opened my eyes. It was half past three. I kept awake thinking about this dream until I heard a prayer call from a neighbouring mosque.

Balan turned the pages. Under the date, 21 March 1983, Jaffer Sharief had written:

Absurd dreams haunted me last night. At New Delhi railway station, officials including the General Manager and labour union leaders wait for me at the ceremonial entry point. I was to go to Bombay. They are there to see me off. The time is up. My secretary is nervous and clueless. He cannot detain the train nor release it. Passengers are restless. Finally I appeared, half an hour late, in a vintage taxi, wearing a lungi and banian. The dignitaries saluted me. While moving to my saloon, I stopped, pointed to a girl on the platform and ordered that she should join me on my journey to Bombay. Onlookers laughed. She was the Chief Minister of Assam. She readily complied. As the train moved, she announced that she, in fact, was an Ayyangar girl, running a meat shop at Churchgate. Seeing me unmoved, she took out a dagger from her blouse and menacingly inched towards me. I jumped out of the moving train. While rolling along the track, I looked at her. Holding the door bar, she was watching me. Now, she looked like one from the land of pyramids, an Egyptian!

Balan again turned the leaves. The description ran through wayward and haphazard routes. Under the date, 10 May 1984:

Last night, it was virtually a riot of bizarre dreams. While returning from the Parliament, a female followed me to my flat. She started telling her story, sitting across the table in my room sipping a glass of frothy beer. All of a sudden, the doors of the room opened with a bang and there appeared a robust police officer. His face was red with anger. I sat watching him. The woman got frightened. Though I offered him a seat, he refused. He stood staring at both of us. His right hand rested on the revolver hanging at his waist on the wide leather belt. Slowly but firmly he pulled it out, opened it, counted the bullets, closed again, held it tight, turned towards the female and asked:

'Come with me.'

She looked at me helplessly. I made an attempt to intervene, but he trained the firearm at my chest. He held her hand and dragged her out leaving me alone in the room. I sat numb with my face down. Out in the courtyard, I heard the thundering sound of a shot fired and the screaming of a woman. I smelt gunpowder. I did not venture out. A few moments later, I sensed the approaching footsteps of a person. As I raised my eyes, I saw that person throwing the service revolver on the table with disdain. That person in the police uniform was Amina Bi. I quietly went out and searched the courtyard—there lay a dead cat.

Balan turned leaves. The last entry was against 4 October 1984:

I saw a funny dream in the wee hours of last night. I was the chief guest on the eve of the Republic Day parade. Female battalions participated in march-past group by group. I was the lone spectator in the entire India Gate area. All groups stood for a moment at the saluting base, looked at me through the corner of their eyes and instead of saluting raised their clinched fists and moved away. First it was the turn of air hostesses. There were cadets from Himachal Pradesh and Punjab. Then came the brigade of journalists, politicians and professionals. They had not forgotten their steps. The group of teaching staff from English medium schools and education trusts followed. There was a march-past of divorcees, estranged ones, widows and dependants of those committed suicide by jumping from tops of buildings. I, being tired, began accepting salute lying in an easy chair. Next group was of students from disturbed areas of Kashmir who had joined medical colleges in Karnataka, followed by announcers at railway stations from Madhya Pradesh and singers of gazals in restaurants in Delhi. It was a true reflection of the cross-section of the nation. Finally, the parade of senior citizens took place. I recognized Duggal from Delhi, Guttal from Bangalore and an Ammal from Lucknow. In the last row of that group I noticed the one to whom I had offered bananas in my adolescence. They turned their faces to the opposite side and saluted me with their left hands. One interesting feature that I noticed was that for all these groups, the band was played by a particular team led by a man with a squint.

In the evening, all the groups collected for a get together. The participants approached me batch by batch. Each of them asked,

'Do you remember me?'

I faked ignorance. Among them were cat-eyed witty Jordanians, robust extortionist Egyptians and plump rosy Russians.

They announced in chorus with a glint in their eyes:

'We are your dream mates!'

I observed each of the dream mates who passed me. Their figures had undergone changes. Now they had elongated noses, protruding eyes, distorted teeth, oversized heads and shrunken legs. I laughed, laughed and laughed. Thank God, my wife did not wake up.

Balan, for unknown reasons, did not preserve that notebook but remembered the last sentence: *These truncated dreams are sinful pleasures.*

Shine, how do you read these dreams? An indication of sexual hunger! asked Shade.

In a way it is; but not in the negative sense. Sex is the strongest driving force behind creativity.

Yes, I understand. Genius does exhibit this feature.

You got the point. Jaffer Sharief belongs to that class. Had he not turned to the political field, the society would have got an eminent teacher, an artist or a writer.

At the same time, his failure to stick to a particular company is conspicuous. What does that indicate?

It reflects a sort of discontentment.

Genius, more often than not, gel well with eccentricity. When you flatter him, he will get inflated; ignore him he will shrink; oblige him, he will freeze at the end; resist him, he will lose patience. If you are silly, he will long for a serious mate and if you are intelligent, he will pine for a playmate, said Shine.

You mean to say that satisfaction is alien to a genius? asked Shade.

Well, that is it, concluded Shine.

DIPLOMACY

AT A CERTAIN JUNCTURE in his career, Jaffer Sharief began evincing unusual interest in international affairs. That was not without a reason. Indira Gandhi had deputed him to countries like Iraq, Libya, Saudi Arabia and UAE for lobbying in favour of India's foreign policy. On a couple of occasions, he, as a Union Minister, was made Minister-in-Waiting for a few visiting foreign heads of states. In the process, he befriended personalities like Yasser Arafat and Saddam Hussein. He developed personal equations with some royal family members of the Kingdom of Saudi Arabia. Yet, his real interest lay in the affairs of the east and the west. About Islamic countries, he held the view that they were stooges of America as they were dependants on the latter for defence.

Jaffer Sharief was a bitter critic of American and British administrations for their anti-Islamic stance. He was sad on the day that Yassar Arafat died of ill health. He said it was a western conspiracy and believed that his death had been induced. He was agitated against US President, George Bush Jr, on the day of Saddam Hussein's execution. He called it a cold-blooded murder. Jaffer Sharief brushed aside media reports of atrocities allegedly committed by Saddam on a section of Iranians as cooked up stories by American agents.

Jaffer Sharief almost single handedly organized a protest meet against George Bush and Tony Blair at Bangalore in 2007. Fearing a boost to his image as a spokesman of Muslims, his detractors engaged anti-social elements to sneak into the participating crowd and create turmoil. They succeeded. Violence broke out, arson, stone throwing and looting took place and the police imposed curfew, conducted raids and arrested people. The city was paralyzed. While the protest meet was visibly successful, credit for it evaded Jaffer Sharief as the public attention turned to the unruly events.

Anglo-American anti-Muslim moves had pushed Jaffer Sharief closer to the left political outfits. Worried over the continued bombing and casualties in Iraq, he wrote letters, pen dipped in vitriol, to Bush Jr and Tony Blair.

'Jaffer,' asked a journalist, 'as a keen observer of Indian foreign policy, what do you consider our pinnacle of glory?'

'Liberation of Bangladesh.'

'And, Sharief,' asked another journalist, 'was there any faux pas in our diplomacy which you hate to remember?'

'Rebuff at Rabat! Mr Dinesh Singh, our External Affairs Minister, was India's representative to an Islamic meet at Rabat. No sooner had he landed at Rabat, he staged a hasty retreat without being allowed to even enter the meeting hall for obvious reasons. He was like a character in a play, whom, his otherwise busy wife, deputes to represent her at meetings of the Ladies Club to discuss menopause.'

Long ago, Jaffer Sharief planned his first foreign visit to Singapore. That was around 1975. After securing the passport, visa and air ticket, he had to cancel the trip abruptly, just because Amina Bi vetoed it. Someone in their close circle had conveyed to her that he had picked a female to join the tour, said Shade.

An aborted foreign affair? asked Shine.

'I say, take this down,' Jaffer Sharief called his steno, without lifting his eyes from the newspaper.

'Dear … Harkishan Singhji—'

He had muttered a sound in a low tone, to prefix the name, which the steno could not hear clearly. Usually, it would be 'shri' or 'janab', but this time, it was different. The steno thought that he could retrieve it later. The dictation began:

'I am attaching a copy of my letter addressed to the Prime Minister for your perusal. The topic is the victimization of the Muslim community in the name of terrorism. As leader of the left movement, I am sure that you will understand the sentiments and helplessness of the minority.

'Indeed, it was shocking to read about the explosions in the moving trains in Mumbai. They were heinous acts. I condemn those behind it. However, it is equally disturbing that a whole community has been branded as terrorists just because the investigating machinery doubts certain Muslim extremist organizations. First of all, the doubt has not been substantiated with proof. Secondly, the chances of machinations of the communalists among the major community to tarnish the name of the Muslims have not been taken into account at all. Whenever an incident of destruction takes place, the government agencies, media and the communal outfits start targeting the Muslims.'

'It is sad that on the pretext of suspicion, innocent Muslim youths are being rounded up, detained, interrogated, tortured and then released by the police. They leak the news to the media. Once one is held in the lock-up, one bears the stigma of being a traitor in the society. I have come to know of several instances where marriage proposals for girls have been aborted halfway, thanks to the activism of biased police.

'You are heading a Party that believes in true secularism. Congress has several wolves in sheep's clothing in power. I urge you to take up the anxieties and fears of the miserable Muslim community in Parliament and other forum forcefully. It is shameful for one to have to prove one's patriotism and loyalty to one's own motherland. After all, religion is not a choice, but a chance. Over and above all this, I would remind you that the community, as a whole, is poor and illiterate.

With regards,

Yours sincerely...'

Sinking back into the sofa, waiting for the letter, Jaffer indulged in a monologue:

Sharief, don't you think certain political parties wish that the community remains poor and illiterate for electoral advantage of them? I doubt the motive of the Zacharia Committee too. It could be an agent of the political masters. Its findings serve the purpose of crushing the confidence of the Muslims. The best way to make a community dysfunctional and dispirited is to rob it of its initiative and confidence. The committee advocates state patronage, which virtually is an opium to suppress the vote bank under false hopes.

But, Jaffer, the community in the present political scenario, cannot renounce its claim for protection.

Sharief, we are selling the ownership of the community by opting to be spoonfed. Political poachers thrive on sowing seeds of fear psychosis among our people.

How do you compare Muslims with other communities of similar backwardness?—Sharief asked.

Many of such groups have risen by harnessing their own potential. Look at the Yadavas of the cow belt; Patels of the west; Nadars of the south. They did not wait for state patronage. But Muslims remain poor and illiterate waiting the state to throw breadcrumbs.

You are right, Jaffer. Muslims are gullible. If a Hindu fanatic from Lucknow addresses the Bangalore Muslims in chaste Urdu, they will fall flat, only for that reason.

The steno transcribed the dictation and showed it to him. Jaffer Sharief halted at the salutation. He looked at his steno.

'I said, 'Comrade Harkishan Singh,' and you changed it into Sardar…' correct it and bring it back.

Witnessing the drama, Shade asked Shine:

Why did the steno resent the communist moorings of Jaffer Sharief?

He may be prejudiced. That is not the topic. The question is why did Jaffer Sharief move closer to the comrades?

May I hazard a guess? Asked Shade.

Go ahead, Shine encouraged the Shade.

The Left was at the forefront to argue that the Indian Parliament should condemn the aggression on Iraq. For that matter, the Left argued that India has always condemned aggression.

But Shade, does this argument hold water? Did the Indian Parliament condemn the Soviet invasion of Hungary in 1956; the Soviet invasion of Czechoslovakia in 1968 and the Soviet invasion of Afghanistan in 1979? In the wake of Iraq's invasion of Kuwait, our External Affairs Minister was hugging Saddam Hussein. Yet, the Left insisted that Parliament pass a resolution in support of Iraq, Shine observed.

Perhaps, the Left's solidarity with the Saddam Hussein made Jaffer Sharief pro-Left. However, he conveniently forgot that the very same Left, even today, refuses to admit that it was China that had attacked India in 1962. The massacre of Muslims in Nandigram took place under a Leftist government last year!

All said and done, Jaffer Sharief continues to address his Leftist friends as 'comrades'.

The steno, by nature, had little respect for communists. While changing the salutation, as desired by his boss, he effected one more change at the conclusion, to watch his boss's reaction. Jaffer Sharief went through the revised version. He approved the content. But, when he reached the end, he raised his eyebrows and frowned at the steno.

'I say, you are a funny guy. Who asked you to conclude the letter with 'Lal Salaam'? I am not a cardholder of the Communist Party.'

'Sir, you sounded like one.'

'Listen; there is a limit to taking liberties with me. Produce what I say. No more arguments.'

The steno nodded and returned. On the way, he remembered having read somewhere: for communists, heart is a superstition!

A mischievous brain—Shade and Shine had no doubt.

WRONG/WRONGED

SHADE, YOU ARE AN extension of Jaffer Sharief. As a human being, he could go wrong on men and matters and also be wronged by the surroundings. Do you remember any instances? Shine asked.

Certainly. He has been wrong in his childhood on many beliefs, as any other child would be. He used to watch white and blue pigeons living in the niches of the walls of deep wells or squatting in line on housetops. Seeing the fat pouch under their beaks, he believed that that is where their eggs are produced. That was wrong.

Again, he was fond of speed. He wanted to choose an animal as his vehicle. After several days of observation, his choice fell on a rabbit. He thought that that is the fastest of all carriers on which he could ride. That was wrong.

Yet again, he fantasized on wanting a knife sharp enough to fell trees by running its blade across their trunks as and when he wished. That too was wrong.

Even in his youth he had several such misconceptions. He thought that it was easy to bowl out the opening batsman and difficult to dismiss the tailender. He was under the impression that there will be ten stumps and hitting one of them is much simpler in the beginning than aiming at the last solitary one.

Shade, you are silly to list out such nonsense. These are dreams of innocence. Recollect some of his disappointments or missed opportunities in his career, Shine admonished.

Well, there were occasions when onlookers reaped the crops that Jaffer Sharief sowed, Shade volunteered.

That was not a new happening. In the 1988 Seoul Olympics, Roy Jones Jr of the US believed that he earned the right to have his hand raised as winner in light middleweight boxing. But the referee raised the hand of Park Is Hun of South Korea. After several years, it was proved that the judgment was erroneous, said Shine.

Jaffer Sharief had identical experiences. He rebelled against the governing style of Veerendra Patil, the then Chief Minister of Karnataka. He mobilized public opinion against the state administration. Public and Party workers picked up the thread of protest from Jaffer Sharief. Finally, Rajiv Gandhi, the Congress Prime Minister, removed Patil. But the replacement was not Jaffer Sharief. It was someone else, who had no stronger claim for the chair.

Again, on a couple of occasions, he had agitated against the heads of Karnataka Pradesh Congress Committee. Each time the concerned Party chief had to step down. Such was the amount of pressure exerted by Jaffer Sharief. But at the time of filling in the vacant position, Jaffer Sharief was left out. State Congress leadership continued to be forbidden fruit for him. Later, the seniors confessed that they had been ignoring him deliberately, remarked Shade.

Look Shade, in the case of Roy Jones, one of the judges admitted that he knew Jones had won easily, but he assumed that the other four judges would vote for him. It was to avoid an embarrassment of a 5-0 whitewash for the host country that that judge voted for the South Korean. The tragedy was that two other judges too thought alike! Right after the drug test, according to Jones, the winner, Park, came up to him and said, 'No, I did not win the fight', Shine added.

But Shine, no usurper had ever made any such admission to Jaffer Sharief. However, he did not lose heart, though the sting remained. Instead of carrying this injustice in career into a life of woe-is-me, he won eight Parliament hustling almost consecutively. A period of fifteen years, from 1980 to 1995, could easily be called the purple patch in the career of Jaffer Sharief.

ADVICE

Dear Jaffer,

You have survived violent trials and tribulations in the past. You have faced ignominy, humiliation and isolation. All these have strengthened your faculty to lock horns with impossibilities. You have played your role commendably well. You have carved a niche for yourself in the history of Karnataka. You are on the way to statesmanship.

Sorry for the bluntness of this suggestion: how about your calling it a day? The current field is of bodyline bowling and sledging. Silent voices say that you are on a wet wicket. You are well known for your keen sense of timing. That includes the skill of attack as also the knack of retreat. Umpiring is a boring job; don't opt for that.

In the past, we have seen several ego-driven attempts to come back to activism by many restless seniors. Most of them bit the dust. There was a time when you were unbeatable to the extent that the people complained that the race had become predictable. Do you still have enough motivation to fight? Is the challenge irresistible to you? Remember, there are better ways to serve the society and the community.

Even though you have not said as much in so many words, it is clear that you seek to silence those who scheme against you. It is impossible to turn the clock back and answer the questions that haunted you in the past conclusively.

If you win, that will not be as big a news as if you lose. For defeating you, your critics will spread stories that will do nothing to enhance your reputation. By winning a ninth time, you want to announce that you are not retiring. But better to retire at a time when people ask 'why' and not 'why not'. You already have had a swashbuckling inning. Great musicians wish to stop their concert before their voices turn rough.

All said and done, should you think otherwise, take it for granted that I will be with you.

Good luck!

Yours alternately,

Sharief

NB: See you in the court of justice.

FATE STRIKES AGAIN

MUNNA WAS ADMITTED TO hospital for acute liver dysfunction. He remained there for a week. Jaffer Sharief visited his son twice, nay thrice. First time, he sat by the side of Munna's bed and talked to him. Second time, he saw Munna lying unconscious in the ICU. Third time, the doctors showed him the body of Munna before it was removed to the mortuary. That was on 20 April 2009, four months and ten days after the death of Amina Bi.

Jaffer Sharief was in the midst of an election campaign. He had filed his nomination from Bangalore North Parliamentary constituency. Voting was slated for 23 April. Between Munna's death and voting, there was only a gap of two days. On the 19th, Jaffer Sharief was with his Party workers till well after midnight. Next day, early morning, some relatives woke him up to say that the condition of Munna had worsened. He noticed his family priest among the relatives. As the road was under repair and bumpy and a pain was troubling his back, the vehicle moved slowly. Those who were inside the car were silent. Then Jaffer Sharief's cell phone rang. The call was from a senior Congress leader in Delhi.

'Hello'

'Am I speaking to Jaffer Sharief Saheb?'

'Yes, Jaffer Sharief is on the line,' his tone was even.

After a few moments of hesitation, the caller whispered, 'Condolences.'

Jaffer Sharief could not respond. He was preparing himself

for the worst. The relatives were biding time in breaking the bad news. In the meantime, a certain overactive assistant had flashed the news to Delhi.

Jaffer Sharief accepted the condolences without asking the caller why. That was how the truth befell him.

After seeing the body of his son, he got back into the car. Before leaving, he himself had to give instructions as to the time the funeral procession would start and the spot where his son would be buried.

Inside the car, on his way back home, he went on receiving condolence calls. He nodded to those in the car who conveyed to him that the local media had started telecasting the news. At home, there was a flow of mourners. The body arrived at noon. After it was bathed, it was placed in a coffin in the main hall. The burial took place by evening.

The next day was the last day of open campaign for election. Jaffer Sharief kept away from road shows and public meetings. But he had to move out to give directions to other campaigners as because of a personal loss he was not to leave his workers in the lurch. The next day was the no-public-campaign day when he had to conduct closed-door meetings.

Then dawned the day of voting. Only one half of a total of twenty lakh voters exercised franchise. The Muslim response was lukewarm. Yet, observers and well-wishers assessed that Jaffer Sharief would win with a modest margin. He believed them.

Then arrived the day of counting. That was twenty-two days after the voting. Jaffer Sharief, true to his style, reached the counting centre one hour after the counting began. A few close confidants accompanied him. The initial trend was encouraging to him. He was ahead of his immediate rival by 4,000 votes after the third round of counting. Friends, well-wishers and relatives gathered at different places and remained glued to the television.

'Did I not tell you, Sir? We are winning.' The campaign manager was beaming with joy.

'Keep a close watch of the voting machines. Take care of the needs of our counting agents.'

Jaffer Sharief moved from table to table.

With the fifth round of counting, the lead of Jaffer Sharief rose from 3,000 to 7,000 votes. People started moving towards Jaffer Sharief's house. Flower shops and sweet shops located nearby got ready for brisk business. The lead remained static till the seventh round. In the next round, the lead of 7,000 votes suddenly nose-dived. Now Jaffer Sharief was trailing behind his immediate rival. Panic set in among his supporters. He concealed his tension. After all, it was a seat involving not less than fifteen rounds of counting. There was not much change in ninth and tenth rounds. Suddenly there was an upward surge in favour of Jaffer Sharief in the eleventh round. It almost wiped out the difference. Now both the candidates were at equal level. To the excitement of Jaffer Sharief and his people, the twelfth round gave him a lead of 13,000 votes. Now there could be no looking back. It was impossible to be reversed. All heaved a sigh of relief. Garlands and bouquets started arriving at the house. Jaffer Sharief was confident in his tone while replying to a call from Delhi. He started receiving messages of congratulations in advance. His supporters ran here and there to arrange a befitting victory procession.

Nobody anticipated the shock that lay in store for him. The remaining three rounds completely went in favour of the rival candidate. First the lead began thinning down. The decline was sharp.

'This trend is alarming.'

Jaffer Sharief chanted to himself. Anxiety was palpable. Supporters in the house looked at each other. Mobile phones of those at the counting centres stopped responding.

'Sir, something has gone wrong. We are in for trouble,' a Party worker gathered courage to warn Jaffer Sharief.

'You mean there is no hope.'

'Prepare for the worst.'

'God! You are testing me.' Jaffer Sharief wept in his heart.

Defeat was staring in the faces of the associates of Jaffer Sharief.

The crowd in Jaffer Sharief's house vanished in no time. A pall of gloom set in. Family members switched off the television.

'Unbelievable,' said one of his grandsons.

'I had this fear,' remarked another.

After setting off the advantage, the negative trend overtook Jaffer Sharief. Beginning with 2,000, the lead registered consistent rise and stopped at 35,000 ahead of Jaffer Sharief. That was a big leap. Now, there were no more rounds to be counted. Only tabulation and counting of a few hundreds of postal ballots remained, after which the result would be declared.

Jaffer Sharief was crestfallen. His vision blurred. His throat became dry. He wore a melancholic look. His associates became silent. That was time to retreat. The supporters of his rival candidate were dancing with joy. Jaffer Sharief, accepting his defeat, slowly approached his opponent and congratulated him by shaking his hand. He occupied the backseat of his car. It was half past twelve. As he reached his old house, a few people gathered around his car. He had nothing to talk to them about; nor had they. Through the glass pane of the car window, Jaffer Sharief glanced at the flower baskets and bouquets lying deserted in the corner. He did not get down, but asked the driver to move to his farmhouse, away from the busy city. He slanted to the seat, closing his eyes, hearing the celebrations of the supporters of his rival, all along the route, who were bursting crackers and shouting slogans.

That was the twenty-second day of the death of Munna.

Jaffer, what do you think of my earlier advice? Sharief asked.

No reply.

Do you repent your decision to contest this election?

Jaffer kept mum.

What next?

Jaffer turned his right palm upside with fingers stretched conveying, 'Who knows?'

Remember, you are not alone. You are one of the 540 odd candidates who lost. Two cannot win one seat. Accept the defeat gracefully.

After a pause, Sharief added, we are passing before the burial ground. That is the land of eternal peace. Come on, let us pray for a while.

DIALOGUE UNDERGROUND

COVERING HIS HEAD WITH a handkerchief, Jaffer Sharief stood before the three elongated mounds of earth in the burial ground. Amina Bi was in the middle. She was flanked by her sons—Munna on the right side and Babu on the left. They lay with their heads towards the west. Though it was humid, a layer of static pre-monsoon clouds formed at the centre of the sky mercifully eclipsing the scorching sun. Few crows could be seen. Perhaps, these birds developed a kinship for the visitors of the burial ground. As a frequenter, they knew Jaffer Sharief better. One of them sat on a branch of a nearby neem tree and invited the others. A few collected. They remained there and looked at Jaffer Sharief, fixing each eye on him turn by turn. Crows showed a great sense of family.

In the middle of his prayers, Jaffer Sharief seemed to be picking up signals of an underground communication.

'My sons, here he has come.'

'Why today? It is not Friday.'

'He looks dispirited.'

'He has lost his elections.'

'His dreams of regaining power are shattered.'

'Poor soul!'

'Now, we can look at his losses and gains without passion.'

'That is the advantage of death.'

'Munna, elections overshadowed your death,' Babu commented.

'Elections or no elections, my end was unlikely to disturb any one,' Munna said.

Here Amina Bi intervened.

'But my boy, your life was irretrievable. You were a mere shadow of your old self during the last few years. You had little relevance to the surroundings. Perhaps, you were breathing for my sake; you were waiting for me to walk out first.'

'Ammi Jan, death that does not cause an impact on the survivors is not death. You and I succeeded,' Babu stated.

'Babu, you are right. But as you know, I dislike treading the beaten path. I did not want to hurt or cause discomfort to environment through my death,' Munna noted.

'Yet, they have to pass through the motions of mourning.'

'I can't help it. Those are the demands of the society. In your case, Babu, the shock was real and devastating. Mummy evoked a kind of posthumous pseudo-respect. In my case, it was good riddance.'

Even beneath the earth Munna practised his usual wry humour.

'Despite receiving blow after blow from fate, look, he is fighting. His spirit is commendable,' Amina Bi said.

'That is no wonder. The frog is being gulped by the snake. It is a slow process. Only its head remains to be sucked in. Yet, in that position, the frog stretches its tongue. You know for what? It cannot resist the temptation to catch an insect that flew across its mouth. The world is like that,' Munna, the philosopher, opined.

'Jealousy, greed and ego make the earth unworthy of life,' Babu, the cynic, said drily.

'But, you did not exhibit this wisdom during your days of existence,' said Munna.

'Each emotion is lovely. I was not contented with my spell on earth,' Amina Bi remarked.

'He is concluding his prayers. Tears are rolling down his cheeks,' Munna said.

'He needs someone to take care of him in this old age,' Babu announced.

'Why not he chose a bedmate of his choice?' Amina Bi suggested.

'Mummeeeee...' Munna and Babu screamed together. Their excitement dissolved into silence.

Jaffer Sharief looked towards the sky. The birds suddenly crowing violently fluttered their wings and flew off in different directions like marbles spilled on a smooth surface.

Shine, like a parliament of owls, what is the collective noun for these crows? Shade asked casually.

If I recall rightly...murder.

What did you say, murder?

Yes, a murder of crows!

CROSS-EXAMINATION

YOUR HONOUR, I MAY be permitted to cross-examine the plaintiff who prosecuted me before your Lordship last Friday, Jaffer submitted.

You may proceed, the judge said.

Your name?

Sharief.

Is it a title or a proper noun?

Enlighten me what the difference is.

If it is a title, I must refer to you as 'the' Sharief; if not, 'Mr' Sharief. Now tell the court, who you are.

On record Mr Sharief, but it is a family name.

That means you do not take personal claim to this surname.

I do not claim; nevertheless I wish to.

What is the dictionary meaning of this word?

Honest; straightforward and also decent.

Do you think you live up to the purport of the meaning of this word?

It is up to the society and posterity to assess that.

What says your inner self?

My spirit clashes with my flesh.

Your honour, please take note, Jaffer said.

Do you want your progeny to accept this surname?

Indeed.

Yet if they discard it?

I will feel sad.

What could be the reason for your future generation to reject the surname?

I cannot imagine one.

You are accused of not motivating your successors. What is your comment?

That is unfair.

Is there any truth in this allegation?

Will I ever wish stagnation in the lineage?

It is not stagnation; it is reversal. Mr Sharief, you have set unattainable standards before your successors by your mind-boggling achievements. You are expecting them to jump above the mark that you have conquered. It is frustrating and frightening for them. In order to avoid ignominy and contempt, they escape from the realities of the surroundings. You, being ignorant of this psyche, continue to blame them for inaction. In nutshell, you are responsible for this hopeless situation. What do you have to say?

No comment, said Sharief.

Your honour, please note.

What is your complaint against your alter ego, Jaffer?

Whenever he derails, I attempt to put him back on the right track, but Jaffer resists.

Is derailment frequent?

Yes it often happens.

What are the causes?

Human failure.

Then?

Defective rolling stocks.

Again?

Confusing signals.

Yet?

Worn-out tracks.

If so, could Jaffer alone be blamed for each accident?

Perhaps no, Sharief admitted.

That is all, your honour, Jaffer concluded.

Announcing that the verdict would be handed down next Friday, the learned judge retired. The packed gallery that expected fireworks in the courtroom was stunned by the abrupt closure of the proceedings.

MEMORIES REVISITED

THAT EVENING AN OLD man got down from an auto-rickshaw and waited in front of the big compound gate for permission to enter Jaffer Sharief's palatial building. The security guard, after obtaining a nod, allowed him to walk in. He moved slowly along the fairly long paved path and reached the portico from where someone guided him to Jaffer Sharief's bedroom.

'Oh, Mrityunjaya, you have come to meet me. What a surprise! You move with the help of a walking stick. Look I am bedridden. Did we ever think that we would become so old one day?'

'Never Jaffer. Until the other day, there was a child within me. He used to protest in silence when young people called me uncle and when travellers offered me a seat in a bus, opting themselves to stand. Of late, the presence of that child has started fading out. Today I am not confident of crossing roads and climbing stairs.'

'Mrityunjaya, I have been nursing a desire to visit our school with you. I want to double up along the narrow wet bunds of the paddy fields where we chased crabs and frogs in the rainy season. You were afraid.'

'And you wish to push me into the muddy water again?'

'And you wish to see me being beaten by my mother.'

They laughed heartily.

'Jaffer, one day, while returning from school, we saw a procession of ten to fifteen people shouting slogans against the British. You dragged me into it. I did not know the purpose. After some distance I departed. You continued the march. Next day, our headmaster called us to his room. I was afraid of his cane. But, he lovingly advised us to be careful. Those were the days of the World War. Jaffer, I had been betting on Hitler. It was puzzling to me as to why did you not oppose the British on that issue.'

'Yes, Mrityunjaya, that was a paradox. But by that time, I was getting right directives from my seniors in politics.'

'Okay, Jaffer. But now, don't you bleed when the same Jews who were persecuted by Hitler, torture the Muslims in West Asia.'

'You have raised a valid point. I prefer to believe that an average Jew has no role in the tirade against Muslims. It is the government of Israel that harasses us. Let us return to our childhood. I have none other than you to reminisce with. Do you remember any stories from the textbooks of our last year in the school, Jaffer Sharief?'

'I do. I remember them often. To me the lesson on Shivaji was very interesting. I still have a doubt unresolved. Do you mind if I...'

'Must you be so formal?'

'Jaffer, were you not uncomfortable reading about the anti-Mughal war games of Shivaji. I have watched you drawing silly cartoons without caring for what the teacher said.'

'I don't recollect. The British have distorted Indian history to create a rift between communities. Leave it. We returned from the school telling stories and singing songs. Empty bullock carts used to give us free lifts at times. I prefer to travel in bullock carts than in limousines.'

'Jaffer, don't you remember that incident. It was one summer. We were walking with parched throats. We approached a roadside house for water. An old woman came out with a pot full of water. That was a Brahmin's house. Seeing the sacred thread on my shoulder, she served me water in a brass tumbler. In the meantime she had a searching look at you and asked your name. On hearing your reply, she took a step or two back and keeping that distance she poured water to your palms that you held close to your lips. I was sure that you could not quench your thirst. On the way back, I was shy of talking to you. But you did not allow your ignominy to betray you.'

'Mrityunjaya, I got a chance to take sweet revenge. It was years later. Then I was in power. A grandson of that woman approached me for employment. He was visibly poor. I enquired about his grandmother. She was still alive. I refreshed that experience in my heart.'

Jaffer Sharief stopped for a moment.

'What did you do?' asked the curious Mrityunjaya.

In a low tone, Jaffer Sharief revealed it, as if he had committed a crime.

'I gave him a job in the railways.'

'But Jaffer, you did not wait for that long. On one of the post-school days, you lured a starving girl to the cover of a bush in the village for two bananas. You drew a vicarious excitement in conquering a Brahmin, which she happened to be. I saw her a few years ago, during a train journey. She recognized me, but did not recollect you.'

'Where is she now?' Jaffer Sharief asked.

'No idea. You were un-characteristically restless since the beginning. You could decipher erotic symbols in anything and everything including the dividing point of the branches of the mango tree in the school compound..'

'I have a desire deep in my heart to see that tree once again and watch its present shape. But, who knows whether it has withstood the onslaught of time and weather,' Jaffer Sharief said.

'Some are bestowed with excessive energy,' observed Mrityunjaya.

'Yes, whenever I see a woman with her off-shoots, I used to visualize the moment of her stripping, her posture and her orgasm. Those days are gone forever.'

An attendant brought tea with sugar in a separate pot.

Watching Mrityunjaya adding two spoons full sugar in his tea cup, Jaffer Sharief asked:

'Sugar is not forbidden to you?'

'Not so far, how about you?'

'I have not enjoyed its taste for over sixty years, ever since I was diagnosed as a diabetic. What sin and whose curse—I don't know.'

'Such restrictions affect one's personality. Do you feel bitter at your surroundings?'

'I don't know. But I am jealous of you.'

'I understand; it is not a purchasable pleasure.'

'Jaffer, I visited you for a purpose.' Opening his shoulder bag, Mrityunjaya continued: 'I have been preserving this as a treasure for all these years in spite of shifting my residence several times. I have a desire to gift it to you. You alone could appreciate its value.'

With this introduction, Mrityunjaya pulled out a small bundle and extended it to Jafar Sharief.

'What is this?'

'The textbooks of our school final.'

Jaffer Sharief was stunned. He could not control his emotions. With eyes filled with tears, he received the bundle with both the hands and touched it to his forehead. The classmates were unable to speak for a while.

'These books somehow survived the onslaught of time. Be careful while turning the leaves. You know, I had a habit of colouring the pictures in textbooks with the petals of marigold flowers and teak shoots.'

Jaffer Sharief listened to his friend's directions, closing his eyes.

'Now, Mrityunjaya, tell me about your family?'

'As you know, I have a son and a daughter. I married away my girl to a primary school teacher. My son is working with a travel agency. He owns a taxicab. He looks after me and my wife.'

'Jaffer, I should be leaving now. Who knows when and where we will meet again. Take care. Goodbye.'

As Mrityunjaya turned towards the door, Jaffer Sharief took a glance at his shirt from behind. It was torn below the collar.

'Needs a patchwork,' murmured the tailor in Jaffer.

HE TOO...

DECADES LATER, JAFFER SHARIEF visited the rock-cave of the fakir once again. As he set out, he was unsure of the route to the hill-top. This time there were no pilot and escort. He had been suppressing this urge for a while. Misfortunes, one after the other, had regularly appeared at the threshold of his life bringing with them much grief.

He moved slowly along the busy city streets watching people greeting each other. He grew envious of their spirit and yearned to mingle with them but that was not to be. Along the route, he started arranging the submissions to be made to the fakir in some order—personal losses, aborted opportunities, enforced errors, warring wards. Grievances were craving for precedence. He scribbled them at random on a piece of paper in the moving vehicle.

Jaffer Sharief looked around. Where were the long stretches of dew-drenched grass and soft soil to be covered by foot? The landscape appeared unfamiliar to him. The hill had turned barren and looked denuded. At each pace, an unknown fear engulfed his thoughts. The sky was overcast with darkish clouds that were incapable of delivering rain but successful in blocking light. Eagles were floating in a circular motion overhead. He reached the entrance of the cave and waited there hesitantly for a couple of moments. He removed his footwear and washed his feet, hands and face with the water kept there in a vessel. As he was about to proceed, he saw an old man draped in a torn overcoat approaching him from the side. He came closer and looked at the face of the visitor.

'Fakir saheb?' Jaffer Sharief inquired.

The old man silently started to move, gesturing Jaffer Sharief to follow him. He led the visitor into the interior of the cave. On one side, in the dim light of a flickering oil lamp, Jaffer Sharief saw a six-feet long mound of earth covered with a thick sheet of green cloth. The air was peaceful and fragrant and the silence was meditative. The guide pointed his index finger at the mound.

Jaffer Sharief was not shocked. He had a premonition that something was wrong throughout his journey. Covering his head with a prayer cap, he stood at the feet of the mound and prayed unaware of the passing time. Finally, he took out the piece of paper in which he had listed out his sorrows to be presented to the fakir and tucked it under the sheet near the feet of the saint.

The guide led him outside where the twilight greeted him with a melancholic smile.

'When did it happen?' Jaffer Sharief asked.

'Three months ago.'

'I feel orphaned,' Jaffer Sharief muttered helplessly.

'I understand,' the guide replied.

'Can you give me a souvenir?' Jaffer Sharief pleaded.

'He left nothing behind. He did not use footwear, walking stick or reading glasses.'

'Well, I should be leaving now.' Jaffer Sharief turned around and removed his prayer cap.

'Wait,' the old man said.

He went inside and returned after a while. He held a small packet wrapped in a green piece of cotton cloth in his hand and said: 'You may take it. My days are numbered. Open it only after reaching home. May Allah bless you!'

On his return, Jaffer Sharief said his prayers and then unwrapped the small cloth packet. It contained the string of beads the fakir used for his prayers. He did not dare to touch it. Along with the cloth, he placed the necklace on the stand in front of the smiling portrait of Amina Bi.

A streak of lightening flashed in the horizon heralding rain.

JUDGMENT

THUS CAME FINALLY THE day of judgment. It was a rainy day. A violent storm blew. Deafening thunder exploded.

The court was housed in an old dilapidated building. The tiles over its roof had given away here and there. The room was packed to capacity. Anxious and apprehensive ones occupied doorsteps and windows. They represented all rungs of the society—ragpickers, those with a history of rags to riches, as also the filthy rich. Philanthropists and cutthroats shared seats. Brokers and breakers of peace sat side by side. Practitioners of good and researchers of evil were equally enthusiastic. Preachers of faith and teachers of superstition waited for the verdict at one point. There were hiders of truth and seekers of lies. There were Gandhians, neo-Gandhians, pseudo-Gandhians, anti-Gandhians and un-Gandhians.

In one corner sat Ramu, with his pet, the wounded deer, on his lap. Slowly, a small herd of goats, raindrops dripping from their fur, gathered and took shelter on the verandah. They were the ones whose necks were spared, albeit temporarily, from the hungry blades of swords, thanks to the inclusive motherly compassion of Amina Bi, the commitment for justice displayed by Munna and the instant patriarchic endorsement by Jaffer Sharief.

The hon'ble judge entered, wearing the customary wig of the past. A wave of murmur rose in the air from the gallery. It sounded as if from a beehive.

'Order, order,' the judge hammered mildly on the table. He

then slowly untied the flap of the case file. And without raising his head, the judge read out the verdict:

'After careful consideration of the submissions of the plaintiff and the defendant, and the evidence collected from witnesses, this court adjudges both Jaffer and Sharief to be partly guilty and partly innocent of the accusations. Therefore, both of them are exemplarily punished and honourably acquitted as follows:

A limited length of life of thorns
with blood and bruises is thrust upon!
An unlimited length of life-after-death
of unfading roses and undying glory is granted!

The judge removed his wig and raised his face. Till then the visitors had not noticed him. They were taken aback. The hon'ble judge was none other than:

Jaffer Sharief!

Look here, Shine, the judgment needs no interpretation or elucidation.

That is right. Its message is clear, Shine enlightened, 'Punish the sin, not with death, but with life. One has no licence to elope with death. One has no right to desert one's life. Continue the sojourn, undertake the mission of living as a pilgrimage, halting and starting, till one sees the light.'

Shine and Shade vanished. The wind had calmed down, the thunder had withdrawn, but the rain, alone, continued to sob inconsolably.

FAREWELL

FINALLY, TWO OF YOU have wound up the mission, Ramu said.

Ramu, we feel sad to part with you.

I am afraid I have been showing over-enthusiasm.

A little madness in spring is wholesome even for the king.

Time is up for your departure. Still you have not properly introduced yourself. Shine, who are you?

I am a distant cousin of light. But, keep it in mind I do not possess many of the virtues of that celestial mercy.

And you Shade?

I am a poor novice of the dark phenomenon of shadow. Far be it from me to represent him.

Do you believe that you have done justice in drawing a profile of Jaffer Sharief? asked Ramu.

Our attempt was a creative venture. Absolute satisfaction is a mirage.

Could you have faltered here and there?

We wish we did while identifying the seemingly darker side. We were doing a tight ropewalk.

That means you like your subject.

In fact, we have fallen in love with him.

Look, there he moves sad and drenched along a muddy path with shivering limbs and unsure footsteps, looking towards nothingness. What could be his destination?

He might end up in a frozen valley of silence and loneliness.

Will he adjust?

He is no stranger to isolation. Afterall, it is a self-decreed ordeal. Such courage is rare.

Does he need any help?

He is supposed to be in the good books of the Almighty.

In other words, He alone could help him.

Ramu, do you see—Jaffer Sharief now appears as a tiny black dot, far, far away. A double rainbow has formed in the east against the backdrop of dark clouds gathered there. For that very reason the west has turned out to be breathtakingly gorgeous. And the last ray of the day retreats unwillingly. Just half of its length remains to be pulled back by the western horizon. Once that is over, there is no Ramu, there is no Shade, there is no Shine and there is no Jaffer Sharief either.

And, for us, there is no tomorrow too, added Ramu.

Goodbye!

ACKNOWLEDGEMENTS

I am profoundly indebted to Mr Dibakar Ghosh, Executive Editor of Rupa Publications India, who made me instantly feel at home, in the literal sense of that merciful word!

I am deeply thankful to poet Balendu who displayed monumental patience and enthusiastic indulgence in dressing-up whatever I wrote, rewrote and overwrote!

I am also immensely grateful to Mr K.R. Vinayan, eminent photographer from Hyderabad, through whose camera, I reflect on the cover.

www.ingramcontent.com/pod-product-compliance
Lightning Source LLC
Chambersburg PA
CBHW030809310726
48980CB00006B/433/J
* 9 7 8 8 1 2 9 1 3 8 5 1 4 *